0.81

W9-ATS-682

ATTENTION, READER:

This is an uncorrected galley proof. It is not a finished book and is not expected to look like one.

Errors in spelling, page length, format, etc. all will be corrected when the book is published several months from now.

Uncorrected proof in this form, might be called pre-publicity proof. It was invented so that you, the reader, might know months before actual publication what the author and publisher are offering.

JUMP SHIP TO FREEDOM

JUMP SHIP TO FREEDOM

A Novel by
James Lincoln Collier
and
Christopher Collier

Delacorte Press/New York

Published by
Delacorte Press
1 Dag Hammarskjold Plaza
New York, N.Y. 10017

Manufactured in the United States of America
First printing

LIBRARY OF CONGRESS CATALOGING IN PUBLICATION DATA

ISBN: 0-440-04205-4

For Cricket

Chapter One

I crept up the cellar stairs in the dark, with the bundle of hay in my arms, going as quiet as I could. I figured it was about four in the morning. The door at the top of the stairs was closed, and it was black as black could be, but I'd gone up and down those cellar stairs thousands of times, and I knew them like my own hand.

I had a plan to steal my daddy's money back from Mrs. Ivers. Mrs. Ivers wasn't scared of much, but she was sure scared of fire. She'd talk back to anybody as nasty as could be when she felt like

1

it—the minister, Captain Ivers, anybody. I even saw her talk back to Mr. William Samuel Johnson, who was our delegate to Congress. But she wouldn't talk back to a fire. She was deathly afraid of it, always shrieking at me to be careful with the candles lest I set the curtains on fire and burn the house down or some such. So knowing that, I figured if she thought the house was on fire, she'd run outdoors as fast as she could go, and I'd be able to steal my daddy's money back.

I reached the top of the stairs and laid my hand on the door, just to make sure where it was. The wood was cool on my palm. Even though it was June, it was cool at night down in the cellar where I slept with Mum.

I ran my hand along the wood until I hit the latch, and lifted it up. Then I pushed on the door. It gave a little squeak. I wished I'd thought to grease the hinges the night before with a little tallow or bacon fat. If I wasn't so ignorant I might have thought of it. Probably a white boy would have. But I was black and wasn't as smart as white folks. Leastwise, that's what Mr. Leaming, the minister, always said, although when you got down to it, my daddy was pretty smart, and he was black.

Anyway, I wished I'd thought of greasing the hinges, but there was no help for that now. I had to open the door before I could go through it. So I pushed a little more until it squeaked again, and stopped; and pushed some more, and stopped; and finally I had it open about a foot and I squeezed through into the kitchen.

It was clouded over and there wasn't any moonlight or starlight at all out in the yard. But there was still a few bits of wood glowing in the fireplace, so the hearth was lit up a little—just enough light so I could make out the shapes of the chairs and tables round about the room. For a moment I stood there by the cellar door, back out of the light from the hearth, listening. A couple of times I thought I heard Mrs. Ivers move around in her sleep, but I wasn't sure. Her room was just off the kitchen, backed up against the fireplace. Usually Captain Ivers would have been in there, too, but he was down at the harbor on the brig.

My daddy's money was in the bedroom. Actually, it wasn't real money. It was in soldiers' notes. My daddy got them for fighting in the Revolution. They was worth six hundred dollars—leastwise they would be if Congress voted to pay them off.

A few weeks back, when we found out that my daddy drowned at sea, Mum went and got them out of his safe box. We hadn't hardly come back from the funeral when Mrs. Ivers made Mum give them to her. She said it was for safekeeping, but we knew better than that. Mum should never have let Mrs. Ivers know she'd got them out of my daddy's safe box. My daddy would never have

3

given them over to Mrs. Ivers, but Mum and me belonged to the Iverses and had to do as we was bidden.

I slipped over to the fireplace, moving as quiet as I could, dropped down to my knees on the hearth, and set the bundle of hay down. There was some warmth coming off the fireplace bricks, and it felt good in the cool of the June night. I was plenty scared, though. My arms felt weak and my belly was cold.

My daddy's soldiers' notes was hidden in Mrs. Ivers's Bible, which she kept by her bedside so as to pray over it before she went to bed. It was a stroke of luck for us to find them. A couple of days before, Mum was coming out of the cow shed with the milk. Mrs. Ivers was in the kitchen with Captain Ivers. Just as Mum got up to the door, she heard Captain Ivers say, "Where are they?" and Mrs. Ivers told him, "I put them in the big Bible." Right away Mum knew what they was talking about.

I wished I'd been able to think up a safer plan for stealing them back, though. If I'd have been white, I might have. But there wasn't nothing I could do about that. I knew that black folks were supposed to be more stupid than white folks; that was God's way, the minister said. Black folks were meant to do the work, and white folks the thinking. If God had made black folks smart, they'd have got restless about doing the hard work. Although truth to tell, it never seemed to me that I

4

liked doing the hard work no more than white folks did.

But it was too late to worry about whether my plan would work. I picked up the bundle of hay, and just then I heard a bump from Mrs. Ivers's bedroom. I dropped the hay and jumped up and stood there all scared and frozen. It came to me that maybe I ought to forget about stealing my daddy's money back and all, and creep on back down the cellar before Mrs. Ivers got out of bed and caught me. There probably wasn't much use in it, anyway. The soldiers' notes wasn't going to be worth nothing in Congress didn't vote to change them for real money.

But when I'd got about that far along in my thoughts, a picture of my daddy came into my head. I saw him standing there, tall and stern, and about the bravest man there was until he got drowned at sea, and when I saw him in my head looking down at me there wasn't any way I was going to creep back down those cellar stairs to my bed.

So I listened for a bit, and when I didn't hear anything more from Mrs. Iver's room, I took a soft breath and knelt down on the hearth again. The first thing I did was to divide the bundle of hay in two. I shoved one piece of it up the chimney to block off the smoke from going out. The other bunch I dropped on the glowing coals. The hay cut off the light, making it near pitch dark. I was glad of that, for I felt safer in the dark. Then I leaned forward and began to blow down into the hay to where the coals were, so they'd flare up a little and make the hay catch fire. I kept my mouth down real low and close to the hay so I could blow soft and not make any noise.

The hay began to catch. I didn't want it to flame up, just smolder and give off a lot of smoke, so I reached my hand into the fireplace and clumped it together. By the light from the coals I could see the smoke start to ooze out of the hay in milky curls. I leaned back a little and waved with my hand. The smoke began to waver out into the room. Some of it went up my nose. It burned a little in my throat. I stood up and backed off from the fire, so as not to choke and start coughing. I didn't want to wake up Mrs. Ivers yet.

Mum was down in the cellar, waiting for me to shout. I wondered what she was thinking. For us, those soldiers' notes of my daddy's was freedom. That was the idea of it. My daddy, he got his freedom for fighting in the war, and he figured he'd use his soldiers' notes to buy me and Mum our freedom, too. But the way it turned out, the soldiers' notes wasn't going to be worth anything until Congress decided to give gold or silver for them. So my daddy went to sea to save up some money to buy us free. And then he got drowned, and the only hope we had was the soldiers' notes. Mum figured if we took them down to New York, where Congress was, maybe we could get something for them. We figured Mr. William Samuel Johnson would know what to do, being as he was our delegate and lived here in Stratford.

The smoke was beginning to fill the room pretty good. It was stinging my nose and my lungs a lot, and I knew that in a moment I'd start coughing. So I waited, and held back on the coughs, and then when the room was filled with smoke I let go a good cough as loud as I could. Then I headed across the room, bumping into chairs, and began to bang on Mrs. Ivers's door. "Mrs. Ivers," I shouted. "Wake up, the house is afire."

There came a bumping and a banging, and about two seconds later the door jerked open, and there was Mrs. Ivers with a candle in her hand and her nightcap all twisted on her head. "What's this noise, Daniel?" Then she smelled the smoke. She gave a shriek and busted past me out through the kitchen door into the barnyard.

I slid into her bedroom, waving my arms in front of me so as not to bump into the furniture. I swung around where I figured the bed was, but I guessed wrong and smacked my leg on something. It smarted pretty good.

Outside I could hear Mrs. Ivers tearing around the house to the road, shouting "Fire, fire," to wake up the men down on the brig. I knew she wouldn't come back into the house until she got somebody with her, but the way she was hollering and shouting, she'd wake the dead, and it wouldn't be long before the men on the brig would come running up.

I felt for the bed with my hand and then worked my way around it to the bedside table. The Bible was there. It was big and heavy. I ran my fingers across the pages, and in a minute I hit a crack in them. I flipped the Bible open and felt between the pages, and in a moment I had the notes tucked down under my shirt. Then I felt my way around the bed again and made my way back through the door into the kitchen.

The smoke was pretty thick, making it hard to breathe. My heart was thumping and my hands felt weak and shaky. The hay was beginning to burn now, making that white smoke shine red. I jumped over to the fireplace, pulled the bunch of hay out of the chimney, and dropped it on the fire. Then I grabbed the poker and stirred the hay up to loosen it. In a minute it was flaming up good, and the smoke was being sucked out of the room up the chimney.

I heard somebody say, "Daniel." Mum was standing at the top of the cellar stairs with the door partway open, peeking out. I reached my hand under my shirt, pulled out the notes, and gave them to her. "Good boy," she said. She took the notes, pulled the door closed, and went on down the cellar stairs.

I went outside to clear my lungs. "Mrs. Ivers," I shouted. "Mrs. Ivers, it's all right. The house ain't on fire."

She came up through the dark and peered past

8

me into the house. "Thank God," she said. She was breathing hard, so I knew she was pretty scared. "I was near frightened to death. What on earth happened?"

"It wasn't nothing," I said. "Just an old bird's nest fell down the chimney and begun to smolder."

"My heart's still pounding," she said.

"It wasn't nothing," I said. "Just an old bird's nest."

Chapter Two

My name is Daniel Arabus. I was born in 1773, which made me fourteen in 1787. My daddy was born in 1747. His name was Jack Arabus, and he was a great hero. Once during the war he helped George Washington cross a stream. The way it happened was General Washington was riding along and he came to a stream that had got flooded and risen pretty high and was cutting along fast and muddy over the bottom. The officers figured they'd better dismount and wade across, in case the horses lost their footing.

10

General Washington, he was about to climb down off his horse, but my daddy was right there and he said, "Sir, I know this stream, it ain't as deep as it looks." He took General Washington's horse by the bridle and led it across the stream. General Washington didn't get so much as his feet wet. When they was on the other side, General Washington said to my daddy, "Good work, soldier." And my daddy saluted, and General Washington saluted back.

Honest, it really happened. I heard my daddy tell about it lots of times. George Washington signed my daddy's discharge himself, that's how much he thought of him. I know, because I've seen the discharge myself.

Oh, my daddy, he knew lots of famous men. One of them was Black Sam Fraunces. Mr. Fraunces was a victualler for the army during the Revolution. He bought food for the men. My daddy met Black Sam Fraunces at the Battle of Trenton. They got to be friends. The funny thing was, nobody was sure if Black Sam was a darky or wasn't. He came from the West Indies and spoke French, and he went around bold as you please, the way most darkies wouldn't do. But still, he was black, my daddy said. And he said that someday, after he'd bought my freedom, we'd sign onto a ship headed for New York and he'd take me to meet Black Sam. Black Sam was his friend and would be glad to see him.

Anyway, it was because of my daddy fighting in the Revolution that he got his freedom from Captain Ivers. Leastwise, that was supposed to be the idea of it. But when the war was over, Captain Ivers didn't want to give my daddy up. He wanted him to come back and be his slave some more. My daddy wouldn't stand for that. He ran off, but he got caught and put into jail over in New Haven. So he got a lawyer and sued Captain Ivers in court. The judge said that my daddy was right, and Captain Ivers was wrong. If Daddy fought in the War for the country's Independence, he got his own freedom, too.

But he couldn't get Mum and me free. I never did exactly understand why his soldiers' notes wasn't worth anything after him fighting so hard for all those years. Why would Congress do that to all those soldiers—white and black—who'd fought and lots of them got killed and their widows and children needing the money?

Anyway, now Mum and me had the notes. After I stole them back from Mrs. Ivers, Mum hid them down in the cellar under her pallet. When she went out to milk the cow, she wrapped them up in a piece of oilcloth, took them out to the cow shed, and hid them in the hayloft, way deep down in the hay. The Ivers never had nothing to do with the cow, except to drink the milk. Mum and me was the only ones who ever went up into the hayloft. The Iverses wouldn't think of going up there and getting themselves covered with dust and cobwebs.

I went out with her. It was just barely day-break. We stood in the half-light amongst the tools and dusty barrels, with the cow crunching away on its hay, and talked about it. "The hard thing to know is if we should sell them off now for what we can get for them, or hang on to them in hopes that Congress votes to pay off the whole value of them."

"When are they likely to vote, Mum?"

"I don't rightly know," she said. "It ain't just the Congress at New York. There's them other men meeting in Philadelphia. They got to decide something about it first."

I didn't know much about it, either. They had formed a convention in Philadelphia to fix up the government of the United States, but being as we wasn't but black folks, nobody told us much about it. "We should ask Mr. Johnson," I said. "He'll know."

William Samuel Johnson was the most important man in Stratford. He was our delegate to Congress. I'd been in his house lots, because my Aunt Willy worked for him. Her name really was Wilhelmina, and she was Mum's little sister. Mr. Johnson's house was a real fancy place, hip-roofed instead of plain gabled like most of them around Stratford. It had three stories and big dormer windows. When I'd go into the kitchen to see my daddy, I could peek into the dining room. There was such a sparkling glass chandelier hanging over the table as you couldn't believe, and a big cupboard just stuffed with silver dishes and mugs and things.

"Yes," Mum said. "He'll help us. He was sorry about your daddy being drowned, and he said to ask him if we needed anything. The only thing is, Mr. Johnson's down in New York at the Congress."

"He comes back sometimes," I said.

"He might not come back for months," she said. "It could be too late."

I knew what she meant by that. There was a lot of talk going around Connecticut about doing away with slavery. A lot of people thought slavery was wrong. Most ordinary white folks didn't own slaves and didn't care one way or another anyway. But the ones that did own slaves, like Captain Ivers, was pretty worried about all that talk. Oh, there wasn't much hope that the legislature would suddenly turn us slaves loose. Slaves was property, and the General Assembly wasn't about to take property away from people—white people, anyway. Slaves was different—they'd already had themselves taken away from themselves. But there was a lot of talk about preventing new slaves from coming into Connecticut, and not letting old ones be sold off South to work in the sugar-cane fields. And any babies that come along now was to be free when they grew up—anyway, that was the

14

law in Connecticut. And naturally that started the white folks who had slaves to thinking that maybe they'd better sell us off while they still had the chance. Mum and me, we knew we was likely to be sold off South. Mum always keeps an ear open to the Iverses, and she'd heard them talking about it.

"Well, I know it might be too late," I said, "but there ain't much we can do about it."

She sighed. "No," she said. "I guess not."

"How soon do you reckon it'll be before Mrs. Ivers finds them notes is missing?"

Mum shook her head. "Tonight, most likely, when she says her prayers."

"Do you figure they'll know it was us who took them?"

"Oh, they'll think so."

"What'll happen?"

She shook her head again. "I just don't know."

Then Mrs. Ivers hollered out that I was to go down to the brig and help with the loading. The part of Stratford I lived in was called Newfield. It was just a few houses, two wharves, and Captain Ivers's warehouse, an old wooden building about thirty feet long, with hardly any windows. The main part of Stratford was bigger—lots of houses, and the church where we went on Sundays.

I walked in the dawn down to the landing. The sky in the east was coming up yellow. I liked being in the harbor. I liked the smells of it—the smell of tar and paint and saltwater and fish all mixed together. As I came along, I heard the water lapping quiet against the piles of the wharf where the brig was tied up, its masts as tall as trees and still in the calm water.

I stood there for a minute, looking at it all. Pretty soon I'd have to go aboard, and after that I'd work steady, most likely down in the hold stowing things, where it would be hot as a skillet by eight o'clock in the morning, and half the time you couldn't stand up straight but would have to work bent over or down on your knees, with the boards cutting into your skin.

What I wanted to see was the sun come up out of the sea over across Stratford Point. I always liked that. Standing up there on land, it seemed like when the sun first started to rise up out of the water, you were higher than it. I mean most of the time you think of the sun as being high in the sky, but when you see it rise up or go down in the sea, it seems like it's below you. It gave me a funny feeling, to be higher than the sun.

So I waited, and watched, and in a minute the rim of the sun edged up into sight. Slowly it rose, and gulls wheeled up into the light, shining red and gold, and I stood there in the smell of the tar and paint and saltwater, thinking about nothing but just catching the feeling of it all, and then suddenly I realized that it was plain daylight and I'd better get on board before Captain Ivers came on deck and saw me.

Captain Ivers's brig was called the *Junius*

Brutus. It was maybe seventy-five feet long and pretty broad, about twenty or twenty-five feet across. For cargo you want a broad ship with plenty of room below decks. It was a pretty sight, painted black with a gold band around it. It had two masts, with horizontal yards for the square sails and gaffs and booms for the fore and aft sails. And there were lines going every which way, like a great nest of cobwebs.

Much as I hated Captain Ivers, I sure wanted to sail on the *Junius Brutus* sometime. I wanted to go to sea like my daddy did, and do brave things in storms and such. I used to ask Captain Ivers if I could go as the boy, which was the lowest job, sometime; but he always said no, and I quit asking. If I ever got my freedom, that's what I was going to be—a sailor like my daddy. But there wasn't no use in asking Captain Ivers anymore, so I walked down the wharf and climbed over the rail onto the ship.

The first person I met was Birdsey Brooks, who was Captain Ivers's nephew. He was my age, and we'd gone to school together, except him being white, they figured he was smarter than I was and stayed in school after I stopped so's he could study mathematics and learn navigation. Of course they wouldn't have let no darky study navigation anyway. Still, it made me sort of sore to think that one day Birdsey would be master of a ship, and I would never be no more than a deckhand, even if I was free. My daddy worked on Captain Ivers's ships for years before the war, and he never got to be nothing at all, even though he knew everything about those brigs and could handle one himself in any kind of weather. I knew that, because some of the sailors told me so.

Birdsey was leaning on the rail, eating a chunk of corn bread with molasses on it. "Uncle's been wondering where you was," he said.

"Don't give me none of that, Birdsey," I said. "The sun just come up."

"Well, he's been over at the warehouse cursing you out for near half an hour."

"He'd have cursed me out if I'd got here an hour ago," I said. "Where'd you get the corn bread?"

"Down below. The crew is eating. I come up here to see the sun rise."

I thought of telling Birdsey about the feeling I got when the sun was just coming out of the sea and I was higher than it, but I decided not to. I was afraid that if I said it out plain, it would sound real stupid.

We walked forward to the crew's foc's'l hatchway. The crew's quarters were at the forward end of the ship. At the other end, the stern, the deck was raised up about four feet, and underneath was the captain's quarters, where Captain Ivers and the first mate lived. In between was the big storage hold.

We climbed the ladder down to the crew's quarters. There were double bunks along the wall, some cupboards for stowing gear, and two

18

great anchor chains going straight up from the floor and through the deck above. The men were sitting at a board table eating corn bread and drinking mugs of beer. I was surprised to notice that one of them was Big Tom, a black man who usually sailed out of Stratford. I'd never seen him around Newfield Harbor before. He had muscles in his arms like straps of leather. He'd got a scar running right across his forehead just over his eyebrows, like somebody had tried to slice the top of his head off, and a lot of his teeth was missing. I wondered if he'd been in the Revolution like my daddy, or just got into a lot of fights.

"This here is Uncle's nigger," Birdsey said, pointing to me. "He ain't had any breakfast."

They gave me some of the corn bread and molasses and I went over to a corner and stood there eating it. I knew better than to sit down with the men, even if there was a black man there. Then after a bit the mate hollered down that time was awasting, and we set to work loading the brig.

The way Captain Ivers did business was, he'd buy stuff from farmers in the countryside around and store it in his warehouse until he had a good shipload to trade somewheres—New York or Philadelphia or even the West Indies. Most of the time it was New York. It was only three days' trip, and he knew lots of people there he could trade with. He'd trade in anything—peas, corn, apples, cider. A big part of his business was in livestock, like oxen, horses, cows, hogs, and such. He kept them in pens at the side of his warehouse.

Loading them on the *Junius Brutus* was the worst job of all. There was a big boom which was attached to one of the masts. It had a canvas-and-rope sling at one end and a heavy weight at the other. The idea was to strap a horse or an ox or something into the sling, and heave down on the weight at the other end. The ox would rise right off the ground, kicking and bellowing. Then by swinging the boom around you'd get the ox over the aft hatchway and you could lower it down into the hold. Oh my, the oxen didn't like it at all. They'd thrash around so it was worth your life to get them unstrapped from the sling and hitched to the rings along the side of the storage hold.

Captain Ivers made me and Birdsey work in the hold. We stayed down there all morning, ducking and dodging around those oxen and getting hot and sweaty and stuck up with the hay we were feeding the oxen. By noontime we were pretty tired. We ate our bread and cheese and apples up on the deck in the shade of the quarterdeck over the captain's quarters, feeling the June breeze and watching the sunshine dance on the slow waves coming in across Long Island Sound.

Being with Birdsey made the work go easier. He was a pretty good friend to me, at least as much as a white man can be a friend to a black man.

20

We'd gone to school together and worked a lot together, and climbed the Ivers's apple trees and played hoops and marbles together, only of course I didn't have marbles of my own, they was all Birdsey's, and if I won any I'd have to give them all back at the end. But I didn't mind; he was my friend and it wasn't his fault I didn't have marbles. Working with him made it seem more like I wasn't a slave. Of course Birdsey was going on the ship. He'd already gone on two trips. He was learning to be a sailor.

"I wished I was going with you, Birdsey," I said.

"I wished you was, too," he said. "If you wasn't a slave, you could."

"I'm not always going to be a slave. I'm going to buy me and Mum free."

"Oh come on, Dan," Birdsey said. "That'd cost near a hundred pounds."

"More than that, Birdsey."

"More than that?" he said. "How much do you figure you're worth?"

"Well, my daddy reckoned I'd cost somethin' like eighty pounds to buy."

"Eighty pounds? You're worth eighty pounds?"

"Sure I am," I said. "And Mum probably sixty, because a woman ain't worth as much as a man." That was one thing about being black: I was worth something in pounds and shillings. Most white people, near as I could figure out, wasn't worth much of anything at all. I mean you take a free white man, he was worth maybe twenty shillings a month in wages, and here I was worth about eighty times that just sitting there. "That's why we're worried about getting sold."

"Sold? Why, Uncle wouldn't sell you, Dan." He looked a little uneasy, though, and I could tell he wasn't exactly sure.

"He might," I said. "That's why we want to buy ourselves out first."

"Well, it's going to take you a mighty long time to earn a hundred and forty pounds."

"No, it won't," I said. "We got my daddy's—" Then I caught myself. "I mean, Mrs. Ivers has got my daddy's soldiers' notes for safekeeping. If the Congress makes good on them, we'll have enough."

"What's Congress got to do with it? Soldiers' notes are money, ain't they?"

"No, they ain't. They're just a promise of money. The government don't have to pay off on them if they don't choose to."

"Maybe they won't be worth anything at all, then," Birdsey said.

"That's the point of it, Birdsey. Right now we could sell the notes for something."

"Who'd buy them if they ain't going to be worth anything?"

"Oh, people will buy them cheap on the chance that someday the Congress will pay them at full value. Maybe we could get enough for them to buy one of us free."

22

Birdsey shook his head. "It don't make much sense to me."

"Nor me, neither," I said.

"You ought to ask Uncle about it," he said.

But I wasn't about to do that. We finished eating, climbed back down into the hold, and got the oxen fed and watered. Then we started loading the deck. You didn't waste space on a ship. We lashed stacks of lumber to the deck, tethered more oxen to the railing, put crates of chickens down in the spaces between everything else.

And we was just about finished, along toward twilight, when suddenly I saw Mrs. Ivers on the dock, talking to the captain. I knew what they were talking about right away. The first thought that crossed my mind was to slip over the side and sneak back to the house. But even while I was thinking about it, I knew there wasn't any hope in it. They'd see me, sure.

So I went on working like nothing was wrong, and in a couple of minutes, sure enough, Captain Ivers hollered out, "Arabus, get down here."

"Yessir," I said. I walked to the rail and climbed over pretty slow, not being in any hurry to get down there.

"Quickly," Mrs. Ivers said.

"Yessum," I said. I dropped onto the wharf in front of them. I hardly landed before Captain Ivers hit me and knocked me down hard on the boards.

"Get up," he shouted.

"I ain't done nothing, Captain," I cried, so's they'd think I didn't know what I was getting hit for.

"Get up."

"Yessir," I said. I knelt up and shook my head, like I was sort of groggy. I learned a long time ago that the best thing to do when I got hit was to look as sick and hurt as I could, because nobody likes to bust up a valuable slave.

"Get up."

I got up on my feet and got ready to tilt my head toward him when he swung, so as to take the fist on the top of my head, which would hurt him near as much as me. But they fooled me, for Mrs. Ivers lammed me from the other side instead. My head wobbled, and I fell down again. This time the deck spun around, and I had to sit quiet until I could get steady enough to stand up again. "I ain't done nothing, Captain," I cried out.

"Where are those notes?"

"Notes? I don't know nothing about no notes."

He reached down, grabbed me by the shirt front, and jerked me to my feet. "Don't lie to me boy. You took those notes. Where are they?"

"Honest, I ain't lying. I don't know nothing about them."

He slapped me hard across the face, but he was holding on to my shirt front, so I couldn't fall down. "Answer."

24

"Honest," I said. "I don't know." The one thing was to keep on lying. If he knew I'd taken them, he'd lash me for sure. But so long as he couldn't prove it, he couldn't do more than slap me around a little.

He shook me by the shirt front. "Answer," he said.

"Honest," I started to blurt out, but he belted me across the face again and cut me off in the middle.

Then they made me strip down right there on deck, where the other men could see me. I was dead ashamed to be seen naked that way, especially with the Iverses looking me over and turning me around like I wasn't nothing but a hog ready for butchering. My face and head hurt bad, too, and I had to bite my lip to keep from crying. But after a while they realized that I didn't have the notes hidden on me anywhere, and they let me get dressed again.

Then Captain Ivers said, "Go back to the house and get your old clothes. You're sailing with us in the morning."

I just stared at him. He done just what he wanted. It was a chance for me to take my daddy's soldiers' notes down to Mr. William Samuel Johnson in New York.

Chapter Three

I ran down the wharf and back up the road to the house. Mum was in the kitchen, peeling potatoes with a knife. "Mum," I whispered, even though nobody was around, "I'm going on the brig to New York. Get the notes. I'll take them to Mr. Johnson."

She looked at my face. "The coward hit you pretty hard."

"It doesn't matter," I said. "Get the notes, quick."

But she went on looking at me. "I don't trust

him," she said. "Did he say *why* you was to go on the brig?"

I slowed down and gave that a little thought. "Well, no, he didn't."

"I don't trust him. He wouldn't never take you before. Now he finds them notes missing and all of a sudden he wants you to go."

I began to see that she was right. He had some reason for it that he wasn't telling us. "Well, I ain't got any choice about it, Mum. I have to go. So I might just as well take the notes. We have to take a chance on it."

She thought about it for a minute. "I guess you're right, Daniel. We have to take a chance." She went out to the cow shed to get the notes. I went down into the cellar to gather together some clothes. They didn't amount to very much—just a couple of raggedy shirts and a pair of trousers. About a minute later Mum came down the cellar stairs, with the soldiers' notes tucked into the top of her dress. She gave them to me. I wrapped them up in the clothes and tied the bundle together with a piece of string. "Be careful, Daniel," she said. "He'll lash you sure if he catches you with them."

"I'll be careful. I'll find somewheres to hide them amongst the cargo." Then we heard the front door slam. We came up out of the cellar. The Iverses were standing there. Captain Ivers jerked his head at me. "Arabus, go down and sleep on the brig with the men. We sail at the first tide in morning."

So Mum gave me a big hug, and I hugged her back, and then I said good-bye and left. Saying good-bye to her made me feel kind of peculiar. I was only going for three or four days—a day to sail down and a couple of days to unload and load up again, and a day to sail back. It wasn't a very long time to be away. But I'd never been away from Mum at all, ever, not even for one night. We was very close to each other. My daddy was gone so much at sea or in the army that Mum and me had only each other most of the time. We had to look after each other. We didn't have anybody else. Of course at first, when I was little, Mum was the one who did the looking after. But then when I began to grow some, it came to me that I could look after her, too. Sometimes when Mrs. Ivers put a heavy load of washing on her, and she was likely to go on working into the night, I'd help her so she could fnish in time to get her supper. Or if she got sick, I'd get up before dawn and do her hoeing for her, so she could get some rest. And she'd look out for me the same way. She'd save special pieces of meat for me, so I'd grow up big and strong, and she put aside cloth when she could to make me a warm coat for winter. We looked after each other. We had to. We was all we had.

So it made me feel peculiar, knowing that I wasn't going to see her for a while. But on the other side of it, I was pretty excited about getting a chance to learn how to be a sailor, like my daddy was.

When I got back to the brig, the men were lounging around on deck, taking it easy. Birdsey took me down into the crew's quarters and showed me my bunk and a space in the locker for my spare clothes. With Birdsey standing next to me, there wasn't any way I could unwrap the notes from my clothes and hide them, but in a minute he went back up on deck. I looked around. There wasn't too many hiding places in the crew's quarters. It was going to be safer to tuck them down amongst the cargo when I had a chance. I was thinking about this when Big Tom came down the ladder. Standing up, he looked even bigger, and that scar was bright as a flame in his forehead. He stared at me hard for a minute and then he said, "You're Jack Arabus's boy."

"Yes," I said.

He went on staring at me. "I hear you're a troublemaker."

"Who told you that?" I said.

"Never mind where I heard it. I heard it."

I reckoned it was Captain Ivers who had said that. "Well, it ain't true," I said.

"What happened to them soldiers' notes?"

Then I knew Captain Ivers had been telling him things. Right away I didn't trust him, black or not. "I don't know nothing about them," I said.

He laughed. "Maybe you can get the white

folks to believe your stories, but don't try them on Big Tom."

"Honest, I don't know nothing about them."

"Come on, Arabus, I know you got them, and you know I know. Where'd you hide them?"

I shook my head. "I never touched them. Probably Mrs. Ivers just plain lost them. They wasn't hers anyway."

He stared at me. "Are you saying that Mrs. Ivers stole them notes?"

I sort of blushed. "They ain't hers. They belonged to my daddy."

He stared at me some more. "Now looky here, Arabus," he said in a quiet voice, just in case anyone was listening. "I been shipping out of Stratford for seven, eight years now. I've got me a little money saved, and soon's I get a little more, I'm going to buy me a fishing dory and some nets and set up in business for myself. The one thing I don't want is an uppity nigger causing trouble with the white folks. Things is nice and peaceful between white and black around here right now, and that's the way I want them to stay. If you start a ruckus you ain't going to have trouble just with the Captain, you're going to have trouble with me, too. Understand?"

I looked at him and then I looked down at the floor. But I kept quiet, and in a minute he climbed up the ladder onto the deck, and by and by I went up, too. I reckoned I was lucky that he'd come out that way about the notes, because otherwise I might have trusted him and let something slip.

We sailed the next morning just before dawn when the tide was up, and I began to learn what it was like to be a sailor. It turned out not to be so much fun as I thought it'd be. The idea I had was that you stood around on deck singing work songs, like the ones my daddy used to sing at home, and every once in a while you'd climb up one of the masts to spy out the land or see if there was any whales in the way.

It wasn't like that at all. I tell you, for plain hard work it beat anything I'd ever done. Compared to being a sailor, cutting kindling in the dead of winter when your fingers was like to freeze to the hatchet was a piece of cake. Leastwise, splitting kindling, when you got enough for a few days, you could stop. On a ship, nothing ever stopped.

The main idea of it was to keep the sails trimmed just right so as to take the best advantage of the wind. If there was only a little breeze, you had to keep angling them this way and that to catch the wind the best way. And if you had a good strong wind, you had to take in some sail, which was called furling them, so the ship wouldn't blow over too far and capsize.

Trimming the sails wasn't so bad. There was three big square sails hanging from yards on each mast. Lines ran down from the ends of the yards to places where they could be tied at the railings.

31

To trim the sails all you had to do was ease off on the lines on one side and tighten up the ones on the other.

Furling was the worst job. You had to go right up to the top to do it. They always sent the smallest men up first, because they could slip through the rigging the quickest. Naturally that meant me and Birdsey was always on the jump. The mate would give a shout, and up we'd go, scrambling through the rigging until we got right up to the top.

There wasn't any ladder to stand on up there, nor even a spar—just a big loop of rope that ran along under each sail. So we'd stand on that, me and Birdsey, one of us on each side of the mast, with that line under our feet rocking back and forth, and clinging on for dear life. Only we couldn't cling on with both hands, because we was supposed to be furling the sail, not just enjoying the view. "One hand for yourself, and one for the ship," was the rule, but let me tell you, a lot of times we needed both hands to get that sail furled proper, so we'd cling on with our elbows or legs or whatever part of our bodies we could get ahold of something with, and pray that the ship wouldn't take it in mind to give a sudden lurch.

You didn't want to look down, either. Looking straight out over the sea wasn't so bad. But if you looked down through that mess of rigging, sails, and spars, it seemed like the deck was half a mile away and the men working down there nothing but tiny dolls. I learned quick enough just to race up there, get the job done, and race down again. I mean race, too: If Captain Ivers or the mate didn't think you was moving quick enough, why, they'd blister your skin with their tongues. I never heard such cursing before; it stung like bees.

The other thing was that we didn't wear gloves when we was handling those lines. Gloves was too awkward for tying knots. You just had to let your hands toughen up. Some of those old sailors had calluses thick as boot soles, and about as hard, too. So I let my hands blister up; and then the blisters broke until there wasn't nothing to my palms but raw skin. Oh my, how that stung when I grabbed on to a rope. But there wasn't nothing to do but let it sting and go on with the work. We didn't wear shoes much, either. It was a lot safer walking around on those lines barefooted, so you could get a feel of your footing. And of course my feet began to blister up, too.

Working the sails wasn't all of it, neither. There was the oxen on deck and down below to care for, and the general repairs and polishing to do. On top of it, we had to man the bilge pumps from time to time. When a wooden hull like that creaked and twisted in the wind and waves, the caulking between the planks was bound to work loose. You'd ram the caulk back in and tar it up, but some water was bound to leak in, anyway.

So a couple of days went by. What with the work, and people always being around, Birdsey and I never had much chance to be alone together.

Finally, the second afternoon the brig was out, the mate sent us down to the hold to feed the oxen, and the first thing that Birdsey said was, "Dan, did you steal the soldiers' notes?"

"Who told you that?"

"Everybody knows about it," he said. "Did you steal them? Honest, I won't tell."

"Well," I said, "I ain't admitting nothing, but they was ours by rights, anyway."

"What rights?"

"They was my daddy's," I said. "It was his army pay. He was six years fighting for that money."

"Niggers can't own money," Birdsey said.

"Sure they can," I said.

He thought about that for a minute. "Well, free niggers, sure, they can own money. But not slave niggers. How could a nigger own money if he can't even own himself?"

"You've heard of niggers buying their freedom, haven't you?" I said. "Well, if they couldn't own money, how could they buy their freedom?"

I had him there. "Well, maybe they can own freedom money," he said. But if somebody owns you, it stands to reason that they own whatever you got, too."

That was a pretty good argument. I didn't have any quick way around it. So I said. "Well anyway, those notes are our freedom money. I'm going to use it to buy me and Mum free. When we get down to New York, I'm going to ask Mr. Johnson about it."

31

He stared at me. "New York? What makes you think we're going to New York?"

"Ain't we going to New York?"

"No we ain't. We're going to Stacia."

"Stacia?"

"St. Eustacia. It's an island in the West Indies."

My mouth dropped open, and I stood there just plain dumbfounded. "You mean we ain't going to New York at all?"

"We ain't going nowheres near it, not on this trip. We're going to the West Indies."

Well, I was thunderstruck. I didn't know what to think. I could have sworn I heard Captain Ivers say that the brig was headed for New York, but I couldn't remember clearly. Maybe he never said it and I just reckoned we were going to New York because that was where he most usually went. So my plans were all messed up again, that was for sure. Here I'd got all the risk of carrying those soldiers' notes along with me, and in the end I'd just have to cart them home again, and no closer to getting our freedom than before. Oh, it was a bad turn.

I tell you, it left me pretty down for a while. It just seemed like nothing would go right. First my daddy drowned, and then Mrs. Ivers took the notes away from us, and then me getting hit all over the place for stealing them back; and then when we figure out a plan that might get things to working a little better for us, that goes up in smoke, too. It's bad enough to be born a slave, worse to have hard luck on top of it.

But there wasn't anything I could do about it, so I told myself to cheer up, at least I was learning how to be a sailor. If I learned right, Captain Ivers was sure to take me on other trips, and one way or another I was bound to get to New York sometime. If he didn't sell me off South, first. Besides, it would be kind of interesting to see the West Indies, anyway. So when we was about finished cleaning up the hold, I told Birdsey, "Down there the girls won't look at you twice, Birdsey. They're all black down there. There ain't no white people at all."

"Who told you that?" Birdsey said.

"My daddy. He was down there lots of times. He said it was just like home to him, to see a world full of darkies."

"Oh, I'll bet you there's *some* white folks there," Birdsey said.

"No, there ain't," I said. "Down there the white folks is niggers."

"White folks can't be niggers, you idiot. Even if there ain't no white folks around. It's God's law."

I gave him a grin. "No sir, Birdsey. It's white folks that makes niggers slaves. It stands to reason, if there ain't no white folks, there can't be no slaves." 'Course I knew that wasn't true. Daddy told me often enough that the slaves in the West Indies were treated awful bad. Some places they hardly lived to get old—just died in the cane fields. But I didn't tell Birdsey none of that.

I still had one big problem, which was to figure out where to hide my daddy's soldiers' notes. That night, when I was on watch on deck, I thought about it. If we'd have been going to New York the way I thought, I might have taken a chance on keeping the notes wrapped up in my spare clothes. But now we was going to be at sea at least three weeks going, and three weeks coming back, and who knows how long to sell the cargo and buy one for the return voyage. I couldn't leave them notes lying around for that long, for sure. It was too risky.

It would be easy enough to hide them amongst the lumber lashed to the deck, but if we got a little bad weather, they was certain to get wet and ruined there. The best place, then, was to tuck them into something in the cargo hold. But what?

When my watch was over I came down into the crew's quarters and ate some biscuit. It was quiet down there. Three of the men was lying on their bunks, snoozing. The rest was above deck standing watch. After I finished up the biscuit, I sat quiet for a while, listening to the sleeping men breathe. When I was pretty sure they was sound asleep, I got up. The wall between the crew's quarters and the storage hold was just rough planks, with a door cut into it. I grabbed the lantern off the table and tiptoed through the door.

It was pitch dark in the hold. I waited by the door, listening to make sure that nobody was around. All I could hear was the creaking of the ship and the sound of the oxen chewing and shuffling around. It smelled of dung and hay and tar and saltwater.

When I was satisfied that nobody was in the hold, I held up the lantern. The flame flickered from the wind slipping in through the hatchway, and the shadows of the oxen and bales of hay rocked up and down the walls. Waving that lantern around scared me a good deal. Somebody might spot it, and besides, there was always the chance of setting something on fire. A fire at sea is about the worst thing that can happen. But I had to chance it; I couldn't find a hiding place for the notes in the dark.

I looked around. Toward the stern, near the captain's quarters, there was some boxes and barrels stacked up along the sides. There was grain in the barrels and homespun wool in the boxes. On top of the stack was a fancy cherrywood chest, with a rope tied around it. There was Irish linen in the chest. Captain Ivers figured to sell the chest along with the linen for a good price. It struck me that the linen chest would make a good hiding place for the notes, because they would take extra care of it, being as valuable as it was. It would be easy to untie the rope, slip the notes down among the linen, and tie the rope up again.

I began to creep across the hold, keeping the candle low down as I could. I was about halfway there when I heard voices up top of the ladder that led down to Captain Ivers's quarters. Quickly I blew out the lantern and crouched down behind a bale of hay. A light shone on the ladder, and then some legs appeared, and I knew it was the captain, carrying his own lantern. He climbed on down, and then down behind him came Birdsey. They didn't look in my direction; anyway, I was pretty well hid behind the bale of hay. The captain went into his quarters, and Birdsey behind him.

They shut the door, but they didn't shut it real tight. A rim of light surrounded the door. I could hear their voices, but I couldn't make out what they were saying. I waited, and then I heard the word "Arabus," and I knew they was talking about me. I figured it was about the soldiers' notes. It worried me, all right. Birdsey was my friend, but it worried me just the same.

I lit the lantern again. They wouldn't be able to see it, and anyway, I figured that if they came out and saw me, I'd say I heard a noise and had come in to see if one of the oxen had fallen down. I slipped forward as quick as I dared, through the oxen and hay bales, afraid I'd miss something. In a minute I was crouched outside the door, next to the stack of boxes.

"You understand, Birdsey," the captain said in a muffled voice.

39

"Yes, Uncle."

"On board ship I'm not Uncle, I'm Captain."

"Yes, sir," Birdsey said.

"You understand, then. You're to stay away from Arabus."

"We've been friends since we was little, sir," Birdsey said.

"You're a man now. It was all right to play with the niggers when you were a boy, but not anymore." Then there was a scrape and a thump, like he was moving his chair around, and I missed the rest of what he said.

"Yes, sir," Birdsey said. I could hear him better than the captain. I figured he was standing right by the door, and the captain was sitting in the chair across the room.

"Arabus is a slave. You're the master."

"He might not always be a slave, sir."

"What do you mean by that?" the captain asked.

I held my breath to hear if Birdsey would mention the notes. "I mean, he might buy his freedom or something sometime."

I breathed out. He'd covered up pretty well. "It isn't very likely," the captain said. "He doesn't have any way to raise the money."

I held my breath again. "Lots of niggers buy themselves free, sir," Birdsey said.

"Not so many as you'd think. I wouldn't get my hopes up about Arabus."

They stopped talking for a moment, and there

40

was only the sounds of the ship creaking and the water rushing up the hull. Finally Birdsey said, "There's always a chance."

"No," Captain Ivers said. "There isn't any chance." He'd raised his voice a good bit, and I knew he was losing his temper from Birdsey arguing with him. "No chance whatever. We're not going to discuss this anymore. You're to stay away from Arabus." There came a thump, like he was slamming his hand down on something.

"Sir—"

"Birdsey," the captain shouted. "I have my reasons."

"Sir—"

"Birdsey." Suddenly the captain's voice dropped low, so low that I could only make it out; but I made it out enough. "Birdsey, I'm going to sell Arabus."

"Sell him?" Birdsey sounded pretty shocked.

"When we get to St. Eustacia, I'm going to sell him."

"But why, sir?"

"He's uppity. His father was uppity. It's in the blood."

"Sir, he ain't done nothing wrong that I could see."

"Done nothing wrong? Do you suppose those soldiers' notes flew away on their own? You can't keep a nigger who steals. Arabus is a thief. I can't have him around."

Right then I wished I'd never told Birdsey about

those notes. But he didn't tell; he didn't answer anything at all. "Now, Birdsey," the captain said, "you're not to mention any of this to Arabus. If he finds out that he's to be sold, he'll try to escape, and if he does I'll know it was you who warned him. You have to understand whose side you're on. It was all right playing with Arabus as a boy. But now you're one of us."

I'd heard all I wanted to hear. I crept back down the hold, feeling my way in the dark. I felt cold and sick and wrung out. Being sold off to the West Indies would be terrible. I knew, because my daddy told me. I'd spend the rest of my life bent over and sweating under the sun in the cane fields twelve hours a day, and never see my Mum again, nor be home where I was raised, but live in a strange land with strangers. And as much as I'd miss Mum, she needed me. What would she do? It made me feel so sunk and low to think about it, I wanted to just sit right down there in the hold and give up on everything. What was the point of anything if that was the way I was going to end up? And the question that came into my mind was, would Birdsey tell me about it? Of course I already knew, but would he be a friend and warn me?

Chapter Four

I slipped back through the door into the crew's quarters. The big black sailor, Tom, was sitting at the table, eating biscuit. He gave me a heavy look. "Where *you* been?" He sat there staring at me and chewing his biscuit, that red scar sort of flaming at me.

"Nowheres," I said. "I heard a noise and I thought maybe one of the oxen fell."

He took another bite of biscuit, but he didn't leave off staring. "You ain't been messing with the cargo?"

"No, I ain't," I said.

"Let me tell you something, Arabus. There's sailors who sometimes take it into their heads to set a little bit of the cargo aside for themselves. I've known fellers to hide a little cask of rum under the hay. They figure they'll slip it off in port and sell it themselves. Know what happens to them fellers?"

"No." He wanted to scare me, and he did.

He took another bite of biscuit underneath his stare. "They gets tied to the mainmast and lashed until their backs is red as a slice of beef."

"I wasn't stealing nothing. I told you, I was checking the oxen."

Suddenly he was on his feet and had my shirt front in his hand. He took a quick look to see if the other sailors was asleep. Then he glowered down over me and hissed, "I warned you before, Arabus, I don't want no trouble between white folks and black on this ship. If you step out of line one inch, I'll bust you in half myself."

He was big enough to do it, too. I was mighty scared, and my knees began to tremble.

"I ain't done nothing," I whispered.

He gave me a light slap on my face, so as to sting but not hurt. "That's just a warning." Then he let go and sat down at the table again, eating his biscuit calm as you please.

It just made me feel worse, like the whole world was against me. What had I done, except steal our notes back? It wasn't even stealing. They was our notes. I climbed up into my bunk and lay there staring up at the ceiling. After a while tears began to trickle out and run down my face. I put my hand over my eyes and squeezed them a little, to stop the water leaking out. I didn't want Big Tom to hear me snuffling up there in my bunk. Then I

44

turned on my side and went to sleep.

I didn't see Birdsey again until nearly noon the next day. I was working with the lines, and he was doing one thing and another. I couldn't tell if he was trying to stay away from me or not. At first I thought he might be, but then at lunchtime he came and sat down next to me on the quarterdeck where I was eating and set up a conversation, so I knew he still wanted to be friends. But I knew he wouldn't be able to go against his uncle altogether; he'd have to at least make it look like he was staying away from me.

So we sat eating, and I waited to see whether he would say anything about me being sold off to the West Indies. But he didn't. I figured maybe he was worried somebody might hear.

Then that afternoon the mate sent us down into the hold to work the oxen. It was a good chance for him to tell me; but he didn't, and after a while I realized that he wasn't going to. I didn't know if I blamed him or not. If I ran away, he was bound for a peck of trouble, that was sure. Still, he was supposed to be my friend. He could have told me, and maybe we could have fiugred out a way for me to escape so's he wouldn't get blamed for it.

But he never said nothing. He was going to let me be sold off to the West Indies to work in the cane fields the rest of my life. I remembered what my daddy told me about it: "A man who's used to better couldn't stand working like that day after day. He'd die of the boredom."

45

It made me pretty confused about Birdsey. He was my oldest friend and my best friend, but I couldn't trust him anymore. I wanted to trust him: I wanted to have him for a friend. But I couldn't.

So I didn't have anybody left on my side. It made me feel all cold and lonely. I didn't feel like working, or eating, either.

That afternoon, when I was up in the rigging, it came to me that I could just let go and crash down onto the deck and kill myself. Or take a good jump when the mast rocked over to one side and land in the water and drown.

But then the picture of my daddy came into my head. He sure wouldn't have taken no pride in me if I just up and quit on the whole thing. It wasn't just me; it was Mum, too: it was my job to buy her free, too. My daddy, he got himself drowned trying to buy our freedom. He'd never forgive me if I let the whole thing go without even trying to get loose. Oh, I knew that he was dead and couldn't forgive me one way or another. But it *seemed* like he could. I wanted him to be proud of me, that was for sure.

The first thing I had to do was hide the notes. I waited for my chance, and in the afternoon, when I was off watch, there came a moment when nobody was in the crew's quarters but me. Quickly I unwrapped the notes from my spare clothes and slipped into the hold with them. Nobody was in there, either, and in a minute I had the notes in the cherrywood chest, tucked down amongst the

46

linen.

Then I set about thinking of ways to escape. I had one advantage: I could swim. It was sort of funny, because most sailors couldn't swim. They took pride in it. They figured if your ship went down in a storm, it was best to drown right away and not linger around for a while trying to stay afloat. Swimming was for landlubbers, not for sailors. But me and Birdsey had swum together right as far back as I could remember. There were lots of rivers and creeks around Stratford—the Pequonnock, the Yellow Mill right near the house, and the Housatonic, which was near a mile wide where it came down between Stratford and Milford and out into Long Island Sound. Me and Birdsey used to fish in them and dig oysters in them where they came out into the Sound, and sometimes when it was hot we'd strip down and paddle around, and by and by we just naturally learned how to swim.

So there was that: once we got near to land of some kind, I figured I could slip over the side and swim for shore. It was a pretty scary idea, though: I didn't know how far I could swim. Suppose we anchored a mile out: would I be able to swim that far?

Oh, there were all sorts of complications in it. I mean Captain Ivers was smart; he'd keep a good eye on me when we got close to land, just in case. But I reckoned he couldn't watch me every minute of the day. I was bound to have some sort of chance.

Of course escaping wouldn't put an end to my problems, not by a long shot. There I'd be all by myself out in the middle of some wilderness and no friends to help me out. Oh, I was sorry we weren't going to New York. Mr. Johnson was there, and he knew me from my Aunt Willy working for him. Black Sam Fraunces was there, and he knew me, or leastwise he knew my father. But if I jumped off in the Carolinas or some island in the West Indies, I wouldn't have any friends at all. But I didn't have much choice.

So we went along that day and into the next. According to the mate, we'd got about six hundred miles out. I didn't know how far from land we were, and I didn't want to ask, for fear somebody would get suspicious, but it sure was too far to swim. Besides, the sailors kept saying that these waters was full of sharks. I reckoned they were teasing me, but still, I wasn't much interested in taking a chance.

The next morning the wind began to rise. The sails filled out solid and hard, and the ship began to pick up speed. It was kind of exciting tearing along like that, with the seas charging past the hull and boiling out behind in a long, white wake. But after a while I noticed the captain and the mate standing on the quarterdeck staring off to the south. "Is a storm coming?" I asked Birdsey.

"I don't know," he said. "You're more likely to

see hurricanes later in the season, especially when we get closer to the tropics, but they come up this early sometimes."

By noontime the sky was clouded over, and the sea was running higher. The ship was pitching a good deal, first headlong down into the waves, and then rocking back with the bow up in the air. I was getting nervous, and I wasn't the only one. The men kept looking up at the sky, like an enemy was drifting around up there. We put out the fire in the galley so in case the stove leaned too far, the ship wouldn't catch fire. We nailed the hatch covers down tight, and we put extra lashings on the cargo stowed on deck. If that lumber broke loose and slid across the deck, it could take out lines, the railing, even a mast.

By the afternoon the wind was making a whistling sound in the rigging, and the sky was black as tar. At times sharp gusts of rain would splatter down on us. The oxen tethered to the rail were bellowing and sliding around, and the chickens were flapping in the cages. We took in some sail, but even so the ship raced along, rocking in the high seas. "Why don't we take in more sail?" I asked Birdsey.

"It's a chance to make some time. Uncle likes to push it hard when he can."

We stood double watches that night. It hadn't let up any by morning, and the seas were now rolling and roaring on all sides of us. The ship rocked and pitched, rolling sideways at the same

49

time it rocked forward and backward. About every seventh wave there'd come one that was out of step with the others. It'd hit us by surprise, sort of. For a moment the ship would sort of stop dead and kind of shudder, as if it was trying to shake itself loose. Then it would seem to fall forward, pick up speed, and start the regular rolling and pitching again. You had to hang on to things most of the time to keep your footing at all. The whistling in the rigging was pitched up to a shriek that never stopped. It got on our nerves, just going on and on and on like that. Every once in a while there'd come a great crash of thunder, and a jagged line of lightning would dance down the black sky.

By this time we must have been in the center of the storm, because the wind was coming in gusts sometimes from one side and sometimes from the other. You never knew which way the ship might suddenly lurch or heel. So in the middle of the morning, the mate ordered us to take in most of the sail. I was mighty scared. The way those masts were rocking back and forth, you could easy get shook off into the water. There was no way anybody could save you in those waves: you wouldn't last more than a couple of minutes.

Being smallest, me and Birdsey was up first, headed right to the top of the foremast to take in the top gallant. We started up the rigging side by side, one on each side of the mast, the way we always done it. It was like trying to mount a bucking horse. First the ship would roll to starboard. The mast would tip way over to that side, till it was laying way out over the ocean, with us hanging in the rigging underneath it. Then the ship would rock back. We'd swing up and over, getting slammed around a good bit when it came over the top. Then it would swing all the way down to port, leaving us to hang under the rigging on the other side. Just holding on was hard enough, saying nothing of furling the sail. And all the while down on the deck Captain Ivers was hollering through the wind, "Get moving, get moving," and cursing us out generally. We climbed up and up until we reached the top gallant.

We was now more than fifty feet off the deck, almost at the top of the mast. All around us, as far as I could see out through the dark clouds and the rain, the sea was heaving itself up and down in great hunks, with spray blowing off the tops of the waves in long streamers. Up there, when the ship rocked we seemed to be racing straight down at the boiling water. We wasn't over the ship then: we was hanging way out over the sea, which slashed about below us like it was trying to snatch us out of the rigging and carry us off.

But we wasn't up there just to hang on. Down below, the men were heaving on the lines to pull the top gallant up. Me and Birdsey was on each side of the mast, our bare feet in the rope slung underneath the yard. The rough canvas sail was wet through and heavy as a sheet of lead, except that it was flapping in the wind. We grabbed at it, me and Birdsey, each with one hand, while we hung on to the spar with the other. Slowly we pulled it up against the yard and began tying it up.

Then suddenly the wind gusted. The sail busted out from our grip with a great slap and began to flap wildly like the wings of a huge bird. Me and Birdsey looked at each other. Down on the deck the captain was hollering, but we couldn't make out a bit of what he was saying. We grabbed for the sail, but flapping that way, it was like trying to grab hold of a kicking mule. It kept belting us in the arms and faces, the rough canvas scratching like sandpaper on our skin. My hands were tired and cramped, and my legs getting weak from the strain. It wasn't going to take much for that flapping sail to knock me off my perch.

Then came one of them out-of-step waves. The ship stopped and shuddered. The sail kicked out with a tremendous bang and split across the middle parallel to the yard. The loose ends whipped against my face and chest, and I felt a sting across my cheek sharper than any lash I'd ever got from Captain Ivers. Blood began to drip onto my shirt. We grabbed at the flapping sail and caught enough of it to tie the top half to the yard. My legs and arms were shaking and my face was bleeding and my hands was scraped from the rough canvas. I was soaking wet from the saltwater spray blowing over us. The salt stung in the cuts and scrapes, too. But we wasn't finished, not by a long shot. We had to drop down fifteen feet and do the same thing all over again with the fore topsail.

Oh, it was terrible. But we got the job done. In good weather you ought to be able to furl a sail in two or three minutes, and take in all the canvas on the ship in fifteen. But in the storm it took us more'n half an hour to do it. We left up the main staysail and main topsail. You can't just let a ship drift in a storm; it's liable to get caught the wrong way to a wave and capsize. You've got to be able to steer it up and over the waves. You can't steer a ship if it isn't moving, and it won't move if you don't have some sail up.

By the end of the day, we was all dead tired. It was a whole lot of work just to get from portside to starboard. The oxen wasn't even trying to stand up anymore but just lay there soaked with spray, panting and drooling, with their eyes bugged out. A couple of the chickens, I saw, was already dead in their cages.

It was pretty near impossible to get any sleep with the ship thumping into the waves like that, for you'd hardly doze off when you'd be rolled straight out of your bunk. There wasn't much of anything to eat, either, but cold biscuit. On top of it, we was wet most of the time. You could hardly walk on deck for a minute without getting soaked. Waves was tumbling over the deck, and it was all you could do to find a line to hold on to to keep from washing over the side.

By morning the waves were high as houses. When the ship rode up on top of a crest, we could see out underneath them black skies the water ranged up in moving hills, all dark green and gray and black, with white running 'through it like marble. The next minute we'd cascade down the slope of the wave and we'd be in a valley with the waves standing way above us, and I'd be sure that they would come crashing down on us and capsize the ship and we'd all drown in a minute. But instead we'd ride up the other slope and come up on top of the mountains again.

All the while two or three sailors were wrestling with the tiller, the long handle to the rudder, so as to keep the ship from turning broadside to the wind and the waves. Oh, that was hard work, for the waves had in mind how they wanted the ship to go, and they'd keep twisting it around, and then those sailors would have to heave on the tiller to get her headed back the right way again.

Down below, the oxen were bellowing and staggering around. The mate sent me and Birdsey down there to double up their tethers. If the oxen broke loose they would shift around each time the ship rolled and unbalance it. Of course with all that bending and twisting, the water was coming in through the seams in streams. The bilge pumps had to be manned all the time.

54

We got through the second day of the storm, and the night, too, standing double watches and trying to get a little sleep in between times, with the waves smashing around and the wind roaring and the ship creaking and crackling like it was about to bust in two.

The next morning it was worse. When we slid down into the valleys, it seemed like the waves were near as high as the mainmast, just looming way above us like a great roaring wall. It didn't seem possible that we could stay afloat. During my watch I clung to the rail near the stern, mostly just hanging on, ready to help with the tiller if they needed me. Forward, the oxen lay on the deck, sliding back and forth, too tired even to bellow anymore. They'd slide across the deck as far as their tether ropes would allow, and then slide back again, smacking up against the rail post. Suddenly there came a crack you could hear over the noise of the wind and the waves, and the tiller busted clean in two. The men who were handling it fell to the deck, and the rudder began to flap back and forth, banging on the stern with great heavy thuds. The ship shuddered and swung around into a trough between the waves. Now we had no control of it at all.

Captain Ivers suddenly shot up out of the hatchway, struggled onto the deck, and began working his way toward the tiller, clinging to the railing. "An ax," he shouted. "An ax."

55

I dropped down to my knees, crawled over to the hatchway, and dropped down. There were axes and other tools in a locker in the hold. I worked my way along the wall to the locker, fumbled inside for the ax, and worked my way back topside again. The ship was now broadside to the seas, just bumping and banging and heeling way over after each wave. One of the sailors had got the spare tiller and was clinging to the railing with it, waiting for the stub of the old tiller to be knocked out.

I slid across the deck on my hands and knees with the ax and handed it to the captain. He took a big swing at the place where the broken end fitted into the rudder and knocked the piece out. The sailor slipped the new tiller in place, and the captain banged it to with the butt end of the ax. Then the four of us leaned on the tiller, two on each side, and swung it over. The ship hung there for a minute, and then it came around. Suddenly the sails filled with a slap that you could hear over the sounds of the storm, and we began to move forward again.

Just as we did, I happened to look forward and noticed two of the oxen's tether ropes with nothing attached to them, streaming out in the wind. The oxen had broke loose and slid over the side. I looked back behind us to the roaring sea. There wasn't a trace of them to be seen.

Chapter Five

The storm had been on us now for three days. It seemed like it had gone on forever. I hardly could remember how it had been before, when it was calm and we'd sailed along so easy. It felt like the storm had always been there.

It didn't show signs of dying down, either. In fact, when it began to get lighter on the morning of the fourth day, it seemed to me like the waves was even higher than before, high as the mainmast almost, I reckoned, although it was hard to judge with everything moving every which way all the time.

But I knew they were higher than they were before, because now just about every wave would crash across the deck of the ship, so for a moment we'd be standing in a foot or two of water, all swirling around us, gray-green and foaming, and if we weren't hanging on to something, we'd maybe get washed right over the side. It was awful hard on the oxen. They'd try to struggle up out of the water washing over the deck, staggering and falling all over the place. It was worse for the chickens, though, for the ones in the crates at the bottom couldn't go anyplace but just had to stay underwater for a minute or two until the decks cleared. I could see that more and more of them were drowning all the time.

We stayed on deck most of the time. There wasn't any use in going below to sleep, because it was about as wet down there as it was topside, and we couldn't sleep anyway. So we'd go down only when we was on duty at the bilge pumps, and then we'd try to eat some biscuit and sneak a little rest.

By the middle of the day we knew we were in real trouble. The waves were breaking across the ship regular now. The railing was splintered in a half-dozen places where the oxen had banged into it. Most of the chickens was drowned now, just lying in their cages soggy and dead. One of the oxen had drowned, too, and lay there on deck, his eyes open and his tongue hanging out, sliding back and forth as the ship rolled.

At noontime Birdsey and I went off duty and climbed into the hold to get something to eat and lie down a little. With all the hatches closed but one, it was pretty dark down there. We didn't dare light a lantern, so we sat in the dark eating cold biscuit, feeling wet and miserable and scared.

We was sitting there like that when there came down through the hatchway the voice of the first mate. "Captain," he said. He was standing and he was shouting, otherwise we couldn't have heard him for the wind. "Captain, we're sure to go over if we don't reduce the load. Better cut loose the deck cargo."

We didn't hear anything for a minute except the wind and the waves crashing around, and the creaking of the hull. Then the mate said, "I know it's pounds and shillings, Captain, but it ain't worth drowning for."

Nothing but the storm for a minute; and the mate said, "I'd just as lief let my share go as risk foundering the ship. A share ain't much use when you're at the bottom of the sea feeding the fish."

Then the storm again; and the mate said, "I'm willing to take my risks, sir, but there's risks and risks. Better safe than sorry. I'd just as soon see that cargo cut loose right now."

More storm: "I know you're the captain, sir. I just hope you don't wait too long."

There wasn't anything further after that. Me and Birdsey sat in the dark.

"Birdsey, what's the use of cutting the cargo loose?"

"It lightens the ship, so we'd ride higher in the

water. There's less chance of getting swamped."

"I wished he'd do it, then." I wasn't looking forward to being sold off to the West Indies, but drowning in that boiling sea struck me as worse.

"He won't be in no hurry about it. That deck cargo is worth two hundred pounds."

"It ain't worth much if it's at the bottom," I said.

"It'll hurt business to cut it loose."

It crossed my mind that the crew could throw the captain overboard and say he got washed away in the storm. It would be a great thing for me, because there wouldn't be anybody to sell me off if we ever got to Stacia. And I was about to say so when something stopped me. It was the way Birdsey was talking. It was coming to me that Birdsey was on Captain Ivers's side all the way. He wasn't on my side, he wasn't even on the crew's side: he was on the captain's side.

It kind of bowled me over to realize that. But when I thought about it for a little bit, I could see plainly that I shouldn't have expected anything else. If Birdsey went along with Captain Ivers he stood to do right well for himself. The Iverses didn't have children of their own. Birdsey was the only boy they got. Once he learned his navigation and got a little bigger, he'd get to be mate, and then maybe Captain Ivers would get another ship and make Birdsey captain of it, and after a while Birdsey would end up being a partner in the business and get to be rich, like Mr. Johnson. I'd heard it wouldn't take so long, either:

there was men who was captains when they was eighteen years old.

If you looked at it that way, the deck cargo belonged to Birdsey, too, sort of. It made me see why Birdsey didn't tell me that the captain was going to sell me off. He was on the Ivers's side now, not mine. Oh, I didn't think he wanted me to be sold off; we'd been friends too long for that. But he wasn't going to get himself in trouble with Captain Ivers about it, neither.

It made me feel just so bitter that he'd switched away from me over to the Iverses. But down inside I knew that if it had been me, I'd have done the same. I decided to shut my mouth about throwing Captain Ivers overboard. That was mutiny, and I knew from my daddy that for mutiny a captain could up and hang you from one of the spars on his own say-so. According to the law, on a ship the captain was boss; he could do anything he wanted. Of course no captain was about to hang a person worth eighty pounds, mutiny or no mutiny. But he'd sure lash me down to the bone. I was too tired to think about it, though. We climbed into our bunks and tried to get a little sleep.

I woke up suddenly and found myself sitting in a pool of water. The sea was cascading down through the hatch. "Wake up, Birdsey, we're sinking," I shouted.

But he was already awake and struggling up out

of his bunk. "Let's get out of here," he said.

We staggered through the water sloshing around in the hold and worked our way up the ladder to the deck. The wind was higher than ever, whistling through the rigging like the shriek of somebody being murdered. Rain was driving along almost horizontal, and the spume from the waves was blowing along with it, too. There was so much water in the air it was hard to know if we was under the sea or on top of it. It was near as dark as night, too, but every couple of minutes there'd be a flash of lightning that turned everything into bright day, and right afterward a clap of thunder, like a cannon shot. When that lightning hit, all of sudden we'd see the most tremendous cliff of water standing straight up over our heads. We'd ride up the side of it, with the men on the tiller heaving until their eyes like to bulge out of their heads, and then as we rode up near the top, the wave would break over us and a foot of water would wash across the deck. We was riding too low. Sooner or later one of those waves was going to break before we'd rode up it very far, and we'd be swamped.

The crew were all on deck now and beginning to lash themselves to the railing or the masts or whatever they could. They were all looking back at the quarterdeck, where the mate was standing in front of Captain Ivers, waving his arms and shouting. I couldn't hear what he was saying over the wind and the waves, but Captain Ivers kept shaking his head.

"Tie yourself in," Birdsey shouted. It didn't seem like there was much point in it. We was all going to drown shortly, like enough. Hanging on to the rail, I began to look around for a piece of line. Then two things happened at once. First there was a flash of blinding light, as bright as I'd ever seen, and right on its heels the most tremendous crash that near deafened me. And in the flash of light I saw the pile of lumber lashed to the deck sort of rise up, looking about as big as a house, and come flying across the deck. The next thing I knew the mainmast was falling down on me, with the mainsail flopping and the rigging trailing along behind it like vines. I leapt across the ship and flung myself down on the decking. There was a great smashing, ripping sound. The ship shuddered and began to heel to port. I jumped to my feet and grabbed on to the railing.

The mast was lying at an angle across the ship, with the broken butt end lying just below the quarterdeck and the other end floating way out in the sea. Lying like that, it was pulling the ship over to port; but the broken lines attached to it were all tangled around everything so the mast couldn't slide off. One good wave from the port side would swamp us.

The mate had got hold of an ax and was working his way to the butt of the mast through the mess of lines and splintered wood. A couple of

63

other sailors were coming slowly along behind him. Birdsey and I moved up, too. The mate reached the butt end of the mast and gave it a couple of hits with the ax to free it. Then he began moving up the mast, hacking away at the tangled lines like a man trimming a fallen log. Me and Birdsey and the others grabbed on to the broken end and gave it a heave. We raised it up a foot, but it was still so tangled in the lines we couldn't heave it free. The mate went on hacking.

By now there were cut ends of lines everywhere standing out straight in the air. I snatched at one and wrapped it around my fist, and just then there was another great flash of lightning and I saw standing over us the tallest wave I'd ever seen, like a giant wall. The top started to crumble and cascade down its own side. I squeezed both hands around the line and closed my eyes. The water hit, and I felt myself flung out straight like I'd been belted by a great hand.

I opened my eyes. I was underwater. I gave a couple of heaves with my arms and came up on top. The ship was half underwater, and I couldn't tell if I was on it or out of it. Then I realized that I still had line wrapped around my fist. Just then I felt something bump be. I turned. It was Birdsey, his eyes wide open, his arms waving as he tried to swim against the current washing across the ship. "Help," he cried.

I reached out for him, but he was gone past me,

and then I could only make out the shape of his head in the dark. I felt the ship rise and water race past me as it drained off the deck. At that moment there was another flash of lightning. In the instant of light I saw a confusion of water and railing and loose lines, and that great mast plunging over the side into the swirling sea. And alongside of it went Birdsey, the mate, and two other sailors.

"Birdsey," I cried as the light went out. The ship, freed of the weight of the mast, righted itself. I found myself up against the rail, the line still wrapped around my fist. There came another flash of light. There was two heads in the water staring up at the ship. One of them was Birdsey's. He was looking straight up at me, and his lips was moving. I couldn't hear him over the wind, but I reckoned I knew what he was trying to tell me about. Then the light flicked out, and I stood at the rail all cold and numb, wondering what Birdsey was feeling like out there in the water by himself, drowning. But even while I was thinking that, the thought came to me that with the mast gone and the hull leaking and at least two men missing, there was no way the *Junius Brutus* could make it to the West Indies. Oh, I was ashamed of myself for thinking that with Birdsey out there somewhere trying to keep himself afloat on those terrible waves; so ashamed I came near to jumping in and trying to save him. But I wouldn't do that, I knew. Just then Captain Ivers gave the order to cut loose the deck cargo. But it came too late for Birdsey.

Chapter Six

We pushed the loose planks overboard, untethered the oxen, and drove them through the place where the fallen mast had tore up the railing, and then we heaved the chickens overboard in their crates. Most of them was already drowned, anyway. Riding higher in the water, we lasted out the night, although we had only the one sail on the foremast to work with. By the time the dawn began to turn the sky from black to gray, the storm had begun to ease off. The seas were still running high, great heaving swells rising and falling as far as you

66

could see, but the wind had gone down a good deal and the rain had let up. The hold was two feet deep in water, and a lot more was coming in. The pumps were being manned full-time. We'd ridden her out.

But Birdsey was gone, and so was one of the sailors, washed over the side. The queer thing was that the mate and one of the other sailors who'd been struggling with the mast had got washed over, too; but somehow the water had swirled them back on board again before the ship had risen up, and they managed to grab on to something and save themselves.

We never really knew how it happened. Some said that lightning had hit the mast, busted it off, and that was what jarred the lumber loose. Others said that the lightning didn't have anything to do with it, the lumber had got loose on its own and had cracked the mast when it flew across the deck, so it didn't need but a touch of wind to split it. They said that if the captain had cut loose the lumber, it would never have happened. But there was no way to know for sure.

Captain Ivers never said anything about Birdsey. A day later, when the sky had cleared off and we was dried out a little, he held a funeral service for Birdsey and the other man on the quarterdeck. He just read a little piece out of the Bible and said a prayer. When he got to the part where it said, "Oh Lord, take Birdsey Ivers into Thy care,"

I busted out crying. I was ashamed to cry in front of the other men, but I felt so bad about Birdsey I couldn't help myself. I just had to cry.

Afterward I wondered what Captain Ivers thought about Birdsey dying. Did he feel sick inside? I reckoned he didn't. I reckoned he figured that it was the lightning that done it, and it wouldn't have mattered whether he'd cut loose the deck cargo or not. But he never said anything about it.

The storm had been bad luck for Birdsey, but good luck for me. The *Junius Brutus* was in no shape to go anywheres but straight into the nearest port. We'd got blown a couple of hundred miles back northeast of where the storm hit. The nearest ports were Philadelphia and New York, and the crew figured Captain Ivers would aim for New York, because he traded in New York so much he had friends there, people he could sell the cargo to, and shipyards where he could get the *Junius Brutus* repaired.

"He isn't going to like it, though," one of the sailors said. "He hates to pay that New York impost."

"He'll get around it some way," another sailor said. "He'll anchor out in the harbor and go in himself in the longboat to see if he can talk them into letting him come in for repairs without paying no tax. Then he'll unload on the sly."

I didn't care how he did it. I had finally had

some luck. One we got into New York I'd have a chance to hunt up Mr. Johnson at the Congress and find out about selling our notes. Maybe I'd get a chance to meet Black Sam Fraunces, too. I didn't know exactly how I'd get off ship, but I reckoned I'd find a way. Captain Ivers couldn't keep a watch over me every minute. He'd be busy doing business part of the time, anyway.

The trouble was, I couldn't take pleasure in my good luck, because of Birdsey. Sometimes I'd catch myself thinking about what we would do when we got to New York; how we'd go around together and see the sights. And then I'd remember that he was drowned and I'd get this terrible cold feeling. I'd try to understand what it must have been like for him out there in the water, all alone; but I couldn't. I missed him, that was the truth, even if he wasn't on my side anymore. It helped a lot to realize that when he knew he was drowning he tried to tell me about Captain Ivers selling me off to the West Indies. Of course I couldn't actually hear what he said. But I wanted to believe that he was trying to warn me and I decided I would. There wasn't any good reason not to.

Mainly I tried not to think about Birdsey. I had things of my own to worry about. One big question was what Captain Ivers would do once he had the *Junius Brutus* fitted out again. Would he try to head off for the West Indies again, or would he just give up, sell his cargo for whatever he could get in New York, and head home for New-field? There wasn't any way of knowing; probably Captain Ivers didn't know himself what he was going to do.

Anyway, refitting the ship was going to take some time. She'd need a new mainmast and rigging, some new sails, the railing repaired, the hull caulked where it was leaking, and other things, too. Of course we did some of that work along the way. The way it always was on shipboard, one of the sailors was a carpenter, and he set to work making such repairs as he could with whatever spare planking he could find. But most of the repairs would have to be done in port, and that was bound to take a couple of weeks at least.

But what if Captain Ivers decided to go off to the West Indies, and me with our freedom money hid in the linen chest? That was a problem, all right, for if I found out he was going to do that, I'd have to run away. And then how would I get back to Connecticut to buy Mum her freedom? Besides, running away was risky. You went wandering around on your own all the time, and having to explain to people who you was, and what you were doing. I wasn't much good at making up lies like that. Mum always said things told on my face too much.

So we limped along, going mighty slow with one mast. It took us near a week to reach the New Jersey coast. But finally we sighted the Neversink, a great long cliff on the horizon. Oh, I tell you, it cheered us all up a good deal to see dry land. The sun was shining, there was a nice brisk breeze, and as we got closer we could see trees and even seagulls swirling up and down over the coast.

We pushed along up the coast aways until we came around Sandy Hook into what they call the Lower Bay. Up ahead about ten miles was New York Harbor. To either side, a good distance aways, we could see the green line of land— Staten Island to the west, Coney Island to the east.

According to what one of the sailors said when we was trimming the sails, there was a long sandbar underneath the bay here. "We ought to take on a pilot," he said, "but the old man's too cheap." What we did instead was to tack back and forth for a while, and then by and by along came a big three-masted schooner, near the biggest ship I'd ever seen, and we waited it until it picked up a pilot and then we followed it in across the sandbar. The schooner wasn't the only ship around, not by a long shot. I counted twenty-two of them, coming and going in—big schooners, brigs like the *Junius Brutus*, little sailing craft headed for nearby ports on the New Jersey coast. Once I saw some porpoises, too, leaping around in the water.

A couple of hours later we went through the Narrows, where the land was only a few hundred yards to either side of us. Then it widened out into the Upper Bay, and we eased forward, still limping along pretty slow. About five miles ahead was Manhattan Island, with the North River going off

71

around it to port, and the East River going around it the other way. There was a couple of islands in the bay—Governor's Island to starboard and Bedloe's Island to port. We eased along, and about noon the captain gave the order to drop anchor, and we stopped. We'd made it safe into New York Port.

We was only about a mile off Manhattan Island, and I could see it plain as day, with the windows sparkling in the sunshine. My, it looked big. First there was the Battery, a great stone wall that rose up out of the water to make a sort of end to the island. There was an old fort, too, sitting up on a mound of dirt twice as high as a house. Just beyond the Battery there was a street lined with warehouses, and beyond that I don't know how many houses—thousands, I guess, and a lot of them brick, too. Sticking up through the houses everywhere was church spires, and here and there tall buildings, some of them maybe five or six stories high, near as I could figure. Oh, it got me all excited, knowing that I was looking at one of the biggest cities in America and maybe the whole world, too. I was just as eager as I could be to get off the brig and see it all.

Soon as the anchor was down, Captain Ivers ordered the longboat to be readied so's he could row into the city. "He's going in to argue about the New York impost," one of the sailors said. "He won't bring the brig into a slip until he talks them out of it. I don't blame him none, either. I don't see why Connecticut folk ought to pay duties to New York, anyway. None of the rest of us figure on getting onto land for a spell."

I stood on the deck, looking at the city across the sparkling water, trying to decide what I ought to do. When the captain went, I figured I could slip off the brig just before dawn, swim to shore, see Mr. Johnson, and swim back just before nightfall. It wouldn't be an easy stunt, though. As close as I could reckon, it was a mile, more or less, to Manhattan. I'd never swum a mile, nor anything like it. Swimming around those rivers in Newfield, I'd never done more than a couple of hundred feet at a time. There wasn't any occasion for it.

I looked around to the islands on either side of us. Bedloe's Island, to port, was closest, about a half-mile away, I judged. There wasn't much on it—trees, and on the side facing Manhattan a stone building and a little dock with a small boat tied up to it. I was pretty sure I could swim that far, anyway, and then beg somebody to give me a ride from there into the city.

Still, it was a risk. On the whole, it was probably a better idea to wait until we pulled into dock and watch for my opportunity to skip off for a few hours then.

I was thinking that when the idea came to me that I'd better get the soldiers' notes out of the box of linen I'd hid them in. They'd ridden out the storm fine—I'd checked to be sure—but they was still in that box. I didn't want to risk that box getting unloaded before I could get them out. It was best to do it quick as possible.

So I slipped away from the rail, went forward to the hatchway like I was on some business, climbed down the ladder, and slipped over toward the stack of boxes where the cherrywood linen chest was. There was a nice patch of sunlight shining on the barrels and boxes down there, so I could see my way around pretty well, even out of the sunshine patch. The oxen was on their feet, chewing away, looking like they was enjoying themselves for the first time in a week. I worked my way over to the stack of boxes and started to untie the rope that was around it. Just at that minute a voice shouted, "Arabus," and I knew Captain Ivers had spotted me.

He was halfway down the ladder, looking at me, and I had a hunch he'd seen me come down and had followed me. "What are you messing around with these boxes for?"

"I ain't doing nothing. Captain," I said. "I just came down to see to the oxen."

"You're lying," he said. "I know what you're doing. You're looking for something to set aside to sell for yourself when we dock."

"No, sir," I said. I knew right away that Big Tom had been talking about me. "I wouldn't do nothing like that."

"Don't lie to me, Arabus. You're out to steal what isn't yours."

"No, sir, honest, I wasn't thinking of nothing like that. I just came down to check the oxen."

Suddenly he jumped off the ladder and made a run at me. I ducked, but he caught me on the side of my head, and I fell down between the barrels. Then he grabbed hold of my shirt front, jerked me up again, and the next thing I knew, he had hauled me off into his cabin, stomped out, and slammed the door shut. I heard the key turn in the lock. I was trapped.

It was an awful feeling. Through the little windows in the stern I could see Manhattan Island aglittering away in the sunlight. How was I going to get there now?

I looked around. I'd never been in the captain's quarters before. It was a good-size room for a ship—about fifteen feet square. Underneath the windows was a bunk, covered with a blanket, where the captain and the mate slept—they stood different watches and wouldn't ever be sleeping at the same time. Across from the bunk was a table covered with charts and papers. It had a compass screwed into it. A telescope hung in a rack, and there was a little safe and some casks of rum the captain kept locked up so the sailors wouldn't get into them.

I saw right away that the windows was too small for me to crawl through. I was in a peck of trouble, and I knew it. Oh, I hated Big Tom; it was his doing I was in this mess.

I lay down on the bunk with my hands under my head, staring out the little windows up at the sky. Chunks of white clouds drifted northeastward. In a little while some of them was going to be over Newfield, casting shadows over the harbor, the town, the house, maybe even Mum out in the backyard hoeing the garden patch or hanging up Mrs. Ivers's clothes to dry. I wished I was back there, helping Mum with the washing in the warm sunshine. I wished I was anyplace but where I was.

As I lay there I heard the noise of ropes squeaking in pulleys and I knew they were lowering the longboat into the water. There was some shouting, and splashing. I raised myself up and looked out the window. The longboat was pulling away toward Manhattan. The captain was sitting in the stern. Big Tom was rowing.

Suddenly a suspicion crossed my mind that Captain Ivers was going to sell me as quick as he could. The more I thought about it, the more sense it made. He didn't like me, and he didn't trust me not to run off. On top of it, he was pretty sure I'd stolen our soldiers' notes back. He was bound to figure that I'd got them hidden somewheres back in Newfield and would sell them the first chance I got. Oh, he had a dozen good reasons for getting rid of me, and if those weren't enough, Big Tom would give him some more. Big Tom, he just didn't like any other blacks around. He'd made himself special to Captain Ivers, and he didn't want anybody getting in his way.

I felt about as low as I ever had. I didn't see any way out of it. Captain Ivers would keep me locked up until he'd found somebody to sell me to, and then I'd be carried away in manacles. I'd seen a black man sold like that once. White folks didn't take any chances when they sold you off; they tethered your feet with a short piece of chain so's you could only take little steps. Oh, I felt terrible.

Then all at once in my head I saw my daddy standing up staring down at me. I looked at him, and he looked at me. I knew what he was thinking, too. He was thinking that if he'd been in my fix, he wouldn't have laid there on his back feeling sorry for himself. He'd have got up and done something about it.

I sat up and had a look around. Then I kneeled up on the bunk and studied the little stern windows. They was screwed shut.

I got off the bunk and crossed over to the door. It was solid planking, with two big iron hinges strapped across it. I looked at the hinges. They wasn't screwed down. but bolted clear through the door. There wasn't any way I could get them off, even if I had the tools to do it with.

Then I checked the lock. It was set in the door,

and knowing Captain Ivers, I figured it was a pretty good one and wouldn't be very easy to bust open. I leaned my weight on the door and pressed with my shoulder. The door didn't give at all. I pulled back and gave it a little hit. It still didn't budge. So I backed off and sat down on the bunk and looked around some more—the walls, the windows, and finally the ceiling, which was under the quarterdeck.

There was an oil lamp hanging from the ceiling. I stared at it for a minute, and all of a sudden an idea came to me.

I jerked the woolen blanket off the bed and dumped it onto the floor near the door. Then I unhooked the oil lamp from its holder and poured the oil onto the blanket, spreading it around as much as I could. I looked around for something to light it with. There wasn't anything in sight. I went around behind the captain's desk and pulled open the drawer. There was a flint and steel in a little leather case. I took them out, knelt over the blanket, and began to shower sparks down on the oily places. In a minute a red spot began to glow in the oil. I puffed on it a bit. It began to spread out, a glowing red circle in the wool with wisps of smoke coming up from it. I blew some more. Low, yellow flames began to flicker on the wool.

I stood back and waited. The smoke was rising up and drifting around the room. I backed off farther and climbed up onto the bunk, where I could bust open one of the windows if the smoke got too bad. It drifted up toward me. I coughed and pulled my shirt up over my head to filter out the smoke. It didn't help much. I coughed again and lowered my shirt down.

The smoke was clouding up the room pretty good. I knew that in a couple of minutes I wasn't going to be able to breathe very much. I put my arm over my mouth and nose, jumped off the bunk, snatched the telescope out of its rack, and took a swing at one of the little windows. The glass tinkled and fell out into the water, and the smoke began to ease out of the broken hole. "Help," I shouted. "Fire, fire."

I didn't hear anything for a minute. Then there was a shout and a gabble of voices, and running foorsteps, and in about ten seconds the cabin door flew open and the mate and two sailors was standing there. I dashed toward the door, choking and gasping. The three men came charging in. I bounced off them and nearly fell down, but I managed to stagger past them and race toward the ladder. Behind me I could hear the men cursing and shouting as they stamped on the blanket to put the fire out.

I hit the deck, jumped across it to the railing, and swung over it. Just then I felt a hand grab hold of the back of my shirt. I jerked and let the weight of my body hang out over the water. My shirt pulled free of the hand and then I was falling. I'd got away. But our soldiers' notes were in the linen chest in the hold of the *Junius Brutus*.

Chapter Seven

The water was colder than I figured it'd be, but not so cold as to worry me. I began to swim, striking off toward Bedloe's Island about five hundred yards away. Behind me, from the ship, I could hear shouting. I knew they couldn't catch me. Captain Ivers had the longboat, and none of them on board could swim. I swum along for two or three minutes until I figured I was maybe fifty yards away, and then I stopped swimming, turned around in the water, and looked back. They was all standing at the rail, looking out at me. "Hey, Arabus," the mate shouted. "The old man's going to whip you good when he catches you. You better come back here."

I smiled a smile to myself, which they couldn't see. Then I gave them a big wave. "He's got to catch me, first," I shouted. I turned around again and began to swim at a nice steady pace toward Bedloe's Island.

It took me about ten minutes. I was pretty well blowed when my feet hit bottom, and my arms was tired, but I could have swum farther if I'd had to. It encouraged me that maybe I could make it from Bedloe's Island to Manhattan if I couldn't catch a ride first.

I climbed up out of the water and onto dry land. I turned around again and had a look at the ship. It sat there it the water, pretty still, with only one mast upright. I could see the little shapes of the men still leaning over the rail, trying to spot where I was going. It gave me a funny feeling to think that probably I would never see any of them again.

At the back of the shore there were woods. I walked into them, where they couldn't see me amongst the shadows from the ship, sat down, stripped off my clothes, squeezed them as dry as I could, and put them back on. Then I got up and walked through the woods toward the side of the island facing Manhattan. In a moment I came out of the woods again. There was a small stone house —for storage of some kind, I figured—and a wooden jetty sticking out into the water. Only one boat was tied up there. A man lounged against a post, smoking a pipe.

I was pretty nervous. Coming out of the woods

with my clothes wet like that was bound to make anybody suspicious that I was a runaway. For a minute I thought maybe I shouldn't risk it—maybe I ought to jump back into the water and try to swim to Manhattan Island.

But that was risky, too, so I stepped out of the woods into the sunshine and trotted down to the jetty, trying to look as easy as I could.

The lounger watched me. When I came up to him I said, "Say, you ain't going into Manhattan, are you?"

The lounger took the pipe out of his mouth and puffed out smoke. "Maybe," he said. "Where you headed for?"

His words were sort of slow, and I could smell whiskey, so I knew he was a little drunk. That was all to the good. But I didn't know how to answer his question. I didn't know the names of the streets or anything. There was only one place I knew of, so I said it. "Fraunces' Tavern," I said.

"You work there?"

"I work in the kitchen," I said.

He put the pipe back in his mouth again. "How'd you happen to be out here?" he said.

I should have been ready for that. "Oh, I came out with a boat this morning, and they went off and left me."

The lounger puffed on the pipe. "They just up and left you?"

I wished I'd thought up a better lie. "I was back in the woods there and I got lost and couldn't find my way back," I said. I was beginning to feel prickly and hot.

"You got lost? On an island that ain't more'n half a mile from the water in any direction?"

I blushed. "I ain't very smart," I said.

"No, I can see that," the lounger said. "A smarter liar would remember that his clothes was all wet."

"Oh." I couldn't think of anything more to say.

"Come on, now," he said. "Out with it. You fell off your ship. Which one was it?"

I looked down at my feet and blushed some more, which came pretty easy. "I'll admit it. I was standing watch and I saw a whale or something—leastwise I took it for a whale—and I slung myself out over the railing to get a look at it and I went over."

"I expect you was drunk," the lounger said, taking his pipe out again.

"How'd you guess that?"

"Most times a nigger falls over the side that's the reason. I expect you got into the ship's rum."

"Well, I'll be honest, I ain't much of a hand for drinking. I knew it was going to be chilly standing that early watch, so I had a tot of rum, and that one warmed me up so I figured two would do even better."

He nodded and put the pipe back in again. "I reckon it'll teach you a lesson. What did you say the name of the ship was?"

"The *Housatonic*," I said, which was the name

of a ship from back home. "From Stratford."

"The *Housatonic*? Where's she berthed?"

"Well, that's just it," I said. "Nobody saw me go overboard, so they went on into port. I ain't never been in New York before, so I don't know. Once I found myself in the water, I hit out for the nearest land I could see, which was this here island. I been hiding out in the woods. I was ashamed to show myself. But I'd sure like to get back to my ship."

"You're in for a good hiding, I expect."

"I reckon so, but it wouldn't be the first time. Just so's I get back to my people."

He was convinced. Being a little drunk, he didn't think it out too clearly, anyway. He was heading back across the harbor to Manhattan soon, he said, and if I'd take a turn with the rowing, he'd take me. Provided I didn't get to leaning over the side looking for whales, which was no doubt just porpoises, anyway. And so he did. As I sat pulling on my oar, I thought about how much smarter white folks are than black. Here he'd gone and made up a much better lie than I'd been able to think up myself, without even knowing the circumstances.

So we went on across the harbor and into the East River. I tell you, I'd never seen anything like it in my life. There was ships and boats everywhere you looked, tied up on docks or wharves along the waterfront, and coming and going up and down the river. There was every kind you could think of, from little fishing dories to great three-masted schooners that had been to England and Africa and India and places that you couldn't even imagine.

The lounger pulled the rowboat up to the wharf. "I'll drop you off here," he said. "You go on up and walk along the waterfront. You're bound to come across your ship somewhere along here."

Of course the last thing I wanted was to run into Captain Ivers and Big Tom. I was pretty nervous that they might be somewhere up there on the dockside. But I couldn't do anything about that, so I thanked the lounger, climbed out onto the wharf, and went up onto the street that ran away from the river, it was called Whitehall. I decided I'd better look close at the signposts, in case I had to get back in a hurry.

Oh my, was it busy. It was the middle of the afternoon. There were sheds and stalls and warehouses and shops and inns. And of course thousands of people everywhere—men and women and boys and lots of sailors, some dressed up fine, some drunk and dirty, some racing here and there carrying boxes or sacks over their shoulders, or pushing barrows filled with fish or meat or vegetables through the crowd. And everywhere barrels, boxes, casks, stacks of lumber, crates of chickens, cattle, bales of hay, bundles of cotton. It was all so rich, and busy, and full. Whitehall

85

Street ended and I had to turn. I decided to go right on Dock Street.

Suddenly it came to me that for the first time in my life I was free. I stood there, letting the feeling of it rise up in me. There wasn't anybody around to tell me what to do. I could do whatever I wanted. I could stroll along the waterfront and take in the sights, I could set off for the wilderness, I could walk into one of the warehouses or shops along the dockside, take a job, and spend the money I earned any way that I wanted. Thinking about it, I felt light and sparkling inside. It was just about the sweetest feeling I'd ever had.

But then my worries came over me, and the sparkling feeling went away. The first thing was, I didn't have the soldiers' notes anymore—they was still tucked down inside that cherrywood linen chest on the *Junius Brutus*. The second was that Captain Ivers and Big Tom was certain to be around the waterfront somewhere. If they spotted me, I wouldn't be free anymore, I'd be on my way South to the cane fields. Captain Ivers was bound to reckon that if I ran off once, I'd run off again, and he'd sell me South sure as the moon.

What I had to do was to go to the Congress and find Mr. Johnson. But it was a mighty big city and I didn't have an idea where Congress was.

I was at the corner where Dock Street ran into a great, wide road just full of people and wagons and horses and cows, and even pigs. The signpost said Broad Street. So I slipped back out of the way and stood in the shadows of a long warehouse building, waiting for somebody to come along I could ask directions of who wouldn't ask too many questions back. And in about a minute there came along a little black girl, about ten years old, pushing a barrow filled with oysters. I reckoned she wasn't going to pry too much and wasn't likely to give me away if she got suspicious of me, anyway. As she went by, I grabbed her arm. "Say," I said.

She stopped pushing the barrow and looked at me. "What?" she said.

"I'm looking for the Congress. My master sent me down there with a letter. He told me how to get there, but I forgot. I'm bound for a licking if I don't get there soon."

"I don't see no letter," she said.

"It's in my shirt," I said.

"Who's it for?"

"That ain't none of your business," I said.

"How'd you get your clothes all wet?" she asked.

"You're pretty nosy, ain't you?" She was younger than me. I wasn't going to take anything from her.

"Tell me," she said, "or I won't tell you where the Congress is at."

I'd never met anyone like her for nosiness. "Don't you know it ain't polite to ask all those questions?"

"You asked the first question," she shot back.

"No, I didn't," I said.

"Yes, you did. You asked where the Congress

87

was."

"That ain't the same," I said. Any minute Captain Ivers might come along. "Now tell me or I'll give you a cuff. I can't spend all day talking. I'm bound for a licking as it is."

She didn't say anything for a minute. Then she said, "I don't believe nothing you said. You been swimming around in the harbor. You jumped off your ship and run away."

I grabbed the collar of her gown. "You're a pretty smart dark, ain't you? Now cut out the sass and tell me where Congress is."

She began to squirm around. "I don't know where it is. Let go of my shirt."

"You don't know?"

"I never said I did," she said. She looked at me, worried.

"I ought to cuff you for wasting my time like that. My capt—I could have got into a peck of trouble standing around here."

"It ain't my fault," she said. "I didn't say I knew." She grabbed onto the barrow handles. "I got to go before I get a licking."

"A licking? You ain't likely to get the kind of licking I'll get if they catch me."

"Oh, you don't know," she said. "I work at the most famous tavern in America, and maybe the whole world. They make us step pretty smart."

"What tavern is that?" I said quick.

"Fraunces' Tavern. It's the most—"

I grabbed her by the neck of her gown again.

"All righ', Nosy," I said. "I'm giving you one last chance. You take me to Fraunces' Tavern and I won't cuff you. But no fooling around this time."

It was a stroke of luck. Of course it made me pretty nervous to think about going to see Black Sam Fraunces, being as he was so famous. Maybe he'd forgot all about my daddy. But he was sure to know where Congress was, and maybe how to find Mr. Johnson, too. I had to take a chance on it.

We set off. Nosy turned off from the waterfront, pushing the barrow before her, and I walked alongside. The streets was narrow and crooked and pretty muddy. The houses was right up against the street, and sometimes the cellar stairs cut into the roadway, so you had to watch out. There wasn't so many people coming along here as there was by the waterfront. but the people was made up for by the hogs and cows wandering around loose. There was plenty of dogs, too, and sometimes dead ones lying in the mud.

Finally we came out to where Broad Street met Pearl. "There it is," Nosy said, pointing. I looked down the street. I couldn't believe it. Back home a tavern was about the size of a house, with a bench out front for the loungers to sit on. Fraunces' Tavern was about the biggest building I ever did see. It was made of brick, four stories high with lots of chimneys in the roof, big windows sparkling in the sunshine, and a big fancy door with carvings all around. I could see why Black Sam Fraunces was so famous: I reckoned his tavern was the finest one in all of America. I got more nervous than ever. Why would anybody rich and famous as that take notice of somebody like me, who wasn't anything at all?

Nosy shoved the wheelbarrow along around back. I knew better than to go in through the front door, so I went around back with her. There was a stable there, and a couple of sheds I figured they used for storage, and a well with a big sweep for hauling the bucket up and down. There was people going to and fro in the yard on business— working the stables or carrying food and water in and out of the kitchen. A lot of them were blacks, too.

Nosy shoved the wheelbarrow up next to the kitchen door. "What are you going to do now?" she said.

"I ain't sure," I said. I was good and nervous. It didn't seem right for me just to go in there and barge up to Black Sam Fraunces like he was anybody. "Maybe Mr. Fraunces ain't here?" I wasn't sure whether I was hoping for it or not.

"Oh, he's here all right. He ain't always here, 'cause he sold it, so he goes out to his farm in New Jersey a lot. But he's here right now."

"I guess you probably know what he looks like." I didn't know if I had the nerve for it or not. "I guess you could point him out to me?"

"Why sure I can. Everybody in New York knows him."

"Well listen, Nosy," I said. "You go in there and

90

tell him that Jack Arabus's son is out in the yard, and if he wants to see me he can, and if he don't want to he don't have to."

"Arabus? That's a mighty queer name."

"It ain't any queerer than Nosy."

"Nosy ain't my name," she said. "And if you don't stop calling me that I won't tell Mr. Fraunces nothing about you."

"All right, No—All right, I won't call you it no more. Now you just go on in there and tell him what I said."

"I got to fill this bucket first." So I helped her fill the bucket with oysters from the barrow. She carried it inside, and then I stood there beside the barrow, waiting, feeling mighty nervous. And suddenly I realized that there was a man standing in the door, looking at me.

His skin was dark, there wasn't no doubt of that. Just from looking at him you'd take him for a darky. But he was dressed up mighty fine, in a cockade hat, his shirt all ruffles at the neck and sleeves, and pantaloons the color of ripe plums.

He stepped out of the doorway into the yard, stood there for a minute more, still looking at me. I didn't say anything but just looked back. "Well," he said, "you look like Jack Arabus's boy."

"He was my daddy, sir." I'd never said sir to a black man before. It felt peculiar.

"Was?"

"He drowned, sir," I said. "He went out to sea

in the *Katey Lee* and never came back."

"Drowned?"

"A few weeks ago, sir." I noticed that Nosy had come out of the kitchen and was standing behind Mr. Fraunces, listening.

"Your father was a hero. He deserved better than drowning. That's a cold and lonely way to die."

I thought of Birdsey being flung about by those waves. "Yes sir," I said. "I saw my friend drown on the way down. He didn't like it none. I wished he hadn't." And then all of a sudden I busted into tears. I didn't know why. I stood there crying, not able to stop, and feeling ashamed for weeping so. I put my hands over my face to cover up the tears.

"I knowed you was lying," Nosy said. "You swum off a boat is how you got wet."

"Shut up, Carrie," Mr. Fraunces said. "So, you're a runaway slave? I wonder that your father didn't buy your freedom."

I sort of gasped and got myself together. "He was saving up for it. He was going to use his soldiers' notes for it, but somehow they ain't worth enough anymore, and he had to go to sea to save up for it."

Mr. Fraunces put his arm around my shoulder. "Well," he said, "I guess you better come on inside and tell me about it," he said.

He led me into the kitchen, with Nosy following along behind. It was the biggest kitchen I'd ever

92

seen, with a fireplace you could have stabled horses in, and great pots and pans and kettles hanging down from the ceiling on hooks everywhere. There was a whole hog with its head still on, turning on the spit in the fireplace, and a couple of kettles on hooks over the fire, too. It was getting over toward suppertime now, and two or three men were bustling around, serving up big dishes of stew from the kettles, or chunks of pork and bread. There was waiters in red jackets going in and out. Oh, didn't it smell good in there. I'd been too busy being scared most of the day to think about being hungry, but all of a sudden it hit me.

Mr. Fraunces set me down at a little table off to one side and told Nosy to get me a dish of stew. Oh, it felt mighty warm and comfortable to be there. For the first time in a long, long while I was someplace where it seemed like people liked me. And I wondered if it was because Nosy was black and Mr. Fraunces was black, too. I wished I was sure about that—his being black. But my daddy said he never was sure about him, either, and if my daddy wasn't sure, how was I to know?

Nosy brought the stew, and when I'd got it in front of me and was digging in, I told Mr. Fraunces the whole story—about how Mrs. Ivers stole my daddy's notes, and how I stole them back, and going on the brig, and the storm, and Birdsey drowning, and swimming to Bedloe's Island and coming ashore from there. And when I ended, he just nodded and said, "And what are you planning to do now?"

"I don't know, sir," I said. "I got to get those notes back, somehow."

"And suppose you get the notes?" Mr. Fraunces said.

"I'll take them to Congress and find Mr. William Samuel Johnson, sir. My Aunt Willy used to work for him. He'll help me to sell them."

Mr. Fraunces shook his head. "You're out of luck there, Dan. Some of the men from Congress have gone down to Philadelphia to help rewrite the Articles of Confederation. Mr. Johnson was one of them."

Chapter Eight

It seemed like I was carrying my own bad luck in my pocket. No matter where I went it was there, too, coming along right beside me so as to give me a punch anytime it looked like things were going my way. Here I'd finally made it to New York; but Mr. Johnson was in Philadelphia, and the soldiers' notes was on the *Junius Brutus*.

Mr. Fraunces went off to do some business, and Nosy was set to work opening oysters. I sat there ramming in the food and thinking about my troubles. There just wasn't any way I could sneak on board the brig without getting caught, and once Captain Ivers got hold of me he'd lash the tar out of me, and then sell me off to the West Indies as quick as he could. There wasn't any doubt about that. Nor was there any way for me to get to Philadelphia. If I'd have been white, I could have worked my passage down there in a coastal ship, or even walked down if worse came to worse. But a black boy on his own was bound to raise suspicions that he was a runaway. They generally put out a good reward for runaways. They'd get handbills printed up with a description of me on it, and maybe even a picture, saying fifty dollars reward. Somebody was bound to turn me in. I kept wishing I could thing up some smart plan for getting my notes off the *Junius Brutus*, but nothing came to me. I wondered if Birdsey would have been able to think of something smart.

When I'd rammed as much food in me as I could, I felt a little better. I hadn't had a really good meal since before the storm, and just filling up my belly with fresh bread and hot stew encouraged me a little. I still had my troubles; but at least I felt warm and peaceful for a change. I was mighty sleepy, though, and I just sat there and by and by I dozed off in my chair, and the next thing I knew, Nosy was shaking me. "Hey, Arabus, wake up," she said. "You're supposed to come with me."

I jumped up, shaking my head to get the sleep out of it. "What?"

"You're supposed to come with me."

"Where?"

"Just come along," she said.

I followed her out of the kitchen to a little hall where the back stairs started up. Through a door I could see into the tap room. It was a big room, almost the whole length of the building. There was tables set about, with people eating and drinking, some of them dressed up mighty fine, too, and waiters in red jackets rushing about serving them. The walls had carved paneling, and there was glass chandeliers filled with candles hanging down from the ceiling. Oh, it was the most fancy place I'd ever seen. I wished I could go out there, but the only way I'd ever get into a place like that was if I got to be a waiter and went out there to serve the white folks.

We went on up the stairs, with Nosy asking me the usual questions about where I came from and what it was like for black folks there, and did my daddy really fight in the Revolution, and such. I didn't see any harm in answering, so I did. On up we went, past the second floor and the third one, to the top floor underneath the eaves. We went down a passage to the end, and Nosy knocked on a door. "Who is it?" somebody said from inside.

"It's Carrie, sir. I got Arabus." The door opened, and we went in. It was a little corner room, with two windows looking out south and west. There wasn't much furniture in it—just a bed, a chest of drawers, a couple of chairs, a little table, and a fireplace. Even though it was warm out, there was coals glowing in the fireplace.

Mr. Fraunces was there, standing by the door. Lying in bed propped up on a pillow, with the blankets tucked up under his chin, was an old man. His hair was white, and his wrinkled skin

97

was pale and sweaty. He hadn't shaved, either. It was plain that he was sick, which explained why there was a fire going in the July heat.

Mr. Fraunces shut the door. Me and Nosy just stood there. The old man looked at me. Then he said, "Thou are Jack Arabus's boy?"

"Yes sir," I said.

"Sam says he was drowned. Is that true?"

"Yes sir," I said. "He went out in the *Katey Lee* and they never came back."

"What a pity. He was a fine man. I knew him. I visited him when he was in jail." He began to cough, and stopped talking. There was a glass of rum on the table by the bed, and he took a swallow of it.

It hadn't surprised me too much that Black Sam Fraunces knew about my daddy, because my daddy had told me he knew Mr. Fraunces. But it sure surprised me that this old white man knew him, too. It seemed like my daddy was more famous than I reckoned. It made me feel kind of proud. But there was another part of it, too. From the way the old man said "thou," I knew that he was a Quaker. According to their religion, they wasn't supposed to hurt anybody and was against war. On account of this way of thinking they was against slavery, too, and they was always trying to help out the black folks and some of them even wanted to do away with slavery completely. I figured he knew about my daddy suing Captain Ivers for his freedom.

His name was Mr. Fatherscreft. He asked me a lot of questions, and I told him about stealing our soldiers' notes back, and the storm, and Birdsey getting drowned, and escaping from the brig and the rest of it.

When I got finished, he nodded and lay there thinking for a bit. Then he said, "Well, thou has got thyself in quite a bit of trouble, haven't thee, Daniel?"

"Yes sir, I guess so. I'm worth eighty pounds; Captain Ivers ain't going to let me go easy."

"Eighty pounds?" I'd have thought thee worth more than that."

"Oh, I reckon that's about the going price for a nigger boy."

Mr. Fatherscreft shook his head. "Not in the sight of the Lord, surely. Nor in thy own view, either. I'd have thought that thee would be worth a good deal more than eighty pounds to thyself."

I'd never thought about it that way before. It put a new light on things. "Come to think of it, I suppose I am. If I lived to be pretty old that wouldn't come out to more'n twenty-five shillings a year."

"Thou wouldn't take twenty-five shillings for a year of thy life, would thou, Daniel?"

I shook my head. "No sir. Nor anything near it, neither."

"What would thou take? A thousand pounds?"

I puzzled over that for a minute. "Well, I guess a man's life don't exactly measure out in money. I mean, what's the use of having the money if you don't have your life?"

"That's the point, isn't it, Daniel? Well. Now how dost thou plan to get thy father's notes back from the brig?"

"I don't know, sir," I said. "I hardly even dare go down to the waterfront."

"It would be risky," Mr. Fatherscreft said. He coughed again.

"Where's the brig at the moment?" Mr. Fraunces said.

"I ain't sure. She was anchored off Bedloe's Island this morning."

"You can see Bedloe's from the window," Mr. Fraunces said.

I walked to the window. It was getting dark, but you could plainly see the Battery, the ships tied up at the harbor, and then beyond the Upper Bay with Bedloe's and Governor's islands in them. The *Junius Brutus* wasn't anchored there anymore. "I guess the captain brought her into the dock," I said.

"They'll probably be unloading pretty soon," Mr. Fraunces said. "Ivers will want to get rid of the stuff as soon as possible, so he can put the brig into a shipyard for repairs."

"I've got to get those notes out of there."

"Is it worth the risk, Daniel?" Mr. Fatherscreft asked.

"It's our freedom money, sir," I said.

"It won't be worth much if Captain Ivers catches

thee," he said. "He'll take it away from thee in any case."

"There's Mum. It's her freedom money, too."

Nobody said nothing for a minute. Then Mr. Fatherscreft said, "Suppose the notes turn out to be worthless, Daniel?"

I scratched my head. "I'm blamed if I can see how that could happen, sir," I said. "How could they do that to all those soldiers like my daddy? I mean, he fought and risked his life for years and years. They just wouldn't take his pay away from him, would they?"

"Who dost thou mean by *they*, Daniel?"

"They?" I puzzled over that for a minute. "Why, the government, I guess."

"What government?"

I puzzled about that some more. "Well, come to think of it, I ain't sure. The Congress, I guess."

"But suppose the Congress were to adjourn permanently, just disband entirely."

"What? Just quit?"

"Daniel, the point is this: you've heard of the Philadelphia Convention, surely."

"Oh, yes sir."

"Dost thou know what the convention is doing?"

I thought that one over, too. I was beginning to feel pretty stupid. "Well, sir, not exactly. Captain Ivers says it's to fix up the Articles of Confederation so he won't have to pay import taxes to New York."

"Well, that was the idea, Daniel, but they've decided to scrap the old articles and write a whole new constitution. The greatest men from twelve of the thirteen states are gathered in Philadelphia to try to write a constitution under which all of the states can join into one single nation. But it isn't an easy matter. There are many different ideas about how the new nation ought to work. For example, in a new government, should each state have a single vote in making laws, or should the votes be calculated according to how many people there are in each state?"

I scratched my head again, feeling more stupid. "I don't rightly know," I finally said.

"Neither do the men at the convention," Mr. Fraunces said.

"Thou should understand, Daniel, that the larger states, like Virginia and Pennsylvania, want the votes to be allotted according to population, because that would give them more power. The smaller states, like New Jersey and Maryland, want it one vote to each state, as it is now, so that the large states aren't able to run everything their own way."

"Oh," I said. Once I thought about it, it made sense enough. I could see easy enough that there was likely to be a lot of squabbling over it.

"And that isn't all of it, either, Daniel," Mr. Fatherscreft said. "Some of us are especially worried about what the convention will decide to do about the black people in America. Many of us want slavery abolished. Others, especially the big slaveholders in the South, want slavery continued. Still others have different points of view—slavery should be permitted, but no new slaves brought in; slavery to be permitted in the present thirteen states, but not permitted in any new states that are made, and so forth."

"Do you think they'll set us free, sir?" I asked.

"I don't think there's any chance of that, for now at least. Someday, perhaps. For the present we're trying to bargain for whatever limits on slavery we can get."

"Oh," I said. "Then we'll need our freedom money."

"Yes, of course," Mr. Fatherscreft said. "The point is simply that if the convention fails to agree on all of these questions, they'll give up the attempt to form a new government. Each state will be independent, like the countries of Europe. And the soldiers' notes won't be worth the paper they're printed on, because there'll be no government strong enough to make the states pay taxes. And without tax money, the US government can't pay off the notes."

"They'd be worth nothing at all? After all that fighting my daddy did?"

"Nothing at all. Not a penny. Not unless the state governments decided to pay them. On the other hand, if the convention settles all the disputed points and forms a new federal government, they'll almost certainly pay off the notes—perhaps not in full, but certainly they'll pay something for them."

Once Mr. Fatherscreft spelled it out point by point like that, I could understand it. "If I wasn't just a stupid nigger, I'd have seen it before," I said.

Mr. Fraunces gave me a funny look. "What make you think you're stupid, Daniel?"

My face got hot and sweaty. I shouldn't have said such a thing in front of Mr. Fraunces. Maybe he was black and maybe he wasn't, but whichever way it was, he wasn't stupid. "Well, I guess I am just stupid," I said. "If I'd had more brains I wouldn't have left those soldiers' notes on the brig."

"Seems to me like you had to be pretty smart to get them that far," he said.

That kind of stopped me for a minute. It seemed to me that pretty much everything I'd done had gone wrong. "I don't see what I did that was so smart," I said.

"A lot of people would think that the trick you pulled to escape from the brig was pretty smart."

It confused me. When you figured you was one kind of person all your life, it's hard to start thinking of yourself as another kind. I reckoned I'd have to think about it some more. "If I'd have been really smart I'd have figured out a way to get those soldiers' notes off the brig, too."

104

Mr. Fraunces laughed, and Mr. Fatherscreft gave a little smile, as much as he could, being sick as he was. "Think about it, Daniel," Mr. Fraunces said. "The more important question is, what do you do now? It's my advice to forget about those notes. You don't know what they'll fetch in the end, and it isn't worth taking a chance that you'll spend the rest of your life in slavery to get them."

"They ain't just mine. They're Mum's, too."

"Look, Daniel," Mr. Fraunces said. "As you stand right now, you're free. If you stay out of sight for a couple of weeks, Ivers will be gone back to Connecticut. You could go to Philadelphia or Boston, or west to the new Pennsylvania lands that are opening up, or into the Northwest Territories around Lake Michigan, and start a new life. Why take a chance on it?"

But I knew I couldn't do it. I just couldn't go off like that and leave Mum with no husband and no son, to work for the Iverses all the rest of her life. "I have to get those notes, sir. I know it's risky, but I have to chance it."

"Think about it, Daniel," Mr. Fraunces said. Then he turned to Mr. Fatherscreft. "When do you plan to leave for Philadelphia?" he asked.

"I'm to see William Few tomorrow. If negotiations come right, I'll leave for Philadelphia immediately."

Mr. Fraunces shook his head. "Not as sick as you are," he said.

"I can't let an illness stop me. I'm an old man;

staying alive is of no great importance. It's the work of the Lord that matters."

Then Mr. Fraunces remembered that Nosy and I were listening. "Carrie, find Daniel a place to sleep in one of the sheds. We'll see what to do with him in the morning." So we went and left them talking; but my mind was working, too, for if Mr. Fatherscreft was going to Philadelphia, maybe I could figure out a way to go, too.

Chapter Nine

Nosy found me a place to sleep in one of the sheds back of the tavern, on a pile of empty sacks amongst some bins of fruit and vegetables. I was plenty tired, but worrying as I was about those soldiers' notes, it took me awhile to get to sleep. Finally I dozed off; but when I woke in the morning, I began thinking about them first thing.

I went out of the shed, across the yard, and into the kitchen, hoping that somebody would see how hungry I looked and take pity on me. But the

106

cooks was all dashing around getting breakfast
for the paying guests, and all they said to me was
to keep out of the way unless I wanted a cuffing.
So I went out in the yard and stood there in the
morning sunshine, and by and by Nosy came along
with her barrow. "Where you going, Nosy?" I
said.

"The fish market. They always wants fried fish
for breakfast."

"Well, I'll tell you what, Nosy," I said. "If you
can duck into the kitchen and get hold of a piece
of bread and cheese, I'll go along with you and
give you a hand." There was coming into my mind
the beginning of a plan.

"Maybe I don't need a hand," she said.

"Yes, you do," I said. "But I ain't going to be
very strong if I don't have breakfast."

She gave me a look, but she went into the
kitchen and in a minute came back with a nice
chunk of bread and a big piece of cheese. We went
around the tavern out of the yard into Broad Street
and headed for the waterfront. I chewed on the
bread and cheese as we went along. Naturally,
Nosy began right away asking me questions about
the soldiers' notes and how I'd stolen them back
from Mrs. Ivers, and what they looked like and
what they was worth, until finally I said, "Nosy,
I can't hardly get a mouthful to eat for answering
questions," and she shut up for a couple of
minutes.

We had gone along Broad Street to Dock Street and was getting close enough to the water so's I could smell the smell of it. My nerves was beginning to hum a little. "Now Nosy, where are we coming out to?"

"The fish stalls at Old Slip Market."

"Is that a likely place for Captain Ivers to have docked the *Junius Brutus?*"

She shrugged. "There's no way to know. A lot of them Connecticut captains puts in at Peck's Slip, though. Old Peck, he's a Yankee himself."

I stopped and put a hand on her shoulder. "Now here's the idea, Nosy. If you just amble along the dock with your barrow, maybe you can spot the *Junius Brutus.* You won't have trouble, the railing's all busted up and there ain't but one mast on it. The main thing we have to know is whether they're unloading it. I'm going to wait right here."

"I can't do that. The cook'll kill me if I don't get right back with the fish."

"Oh, come on, Nosy, you ain't scared of the cook, are you?"

"You'd be scared of him too if you'd been cursed out by him as much as I have."

"Oh, a cook's cursing ain't nothing to worry about. Wait till you get cursed out by a mate. That's real cursing."

"Well, I ain't going to do it," she said. "You didn't say nothing about it when we left."

"Oh, you'll do it, Nosy. Because if I do it on my

108

own, you'll be left out, and I won't tell you none of it afterward. You'll never know what I did."

That got to her, I could see that. She kind of swung her eyes around here and there, and finally she said, "Well, just for a little bit," she said. "Then I got to get back with the fish."

"I knew you'd do it, Nosy. I knew you wasn't a coward."

She trotted off, and I ducked back into a little alleyway where I was covered in shadows, and waited. I was pretty sure she wouldn't stop looking until she found the brig. She was too curious to quit until she'd seen what it looked like and knew what was going on.

So I waited; and waited; and about twenty minutes later she came trotting back with the barrow loaded up with fish, all out of breath. "I seen it," she said. "The mainmast was busted clean off."

"I already knew that, Nosy. Where's she at?"

"Peck's Slip, like I said."

"Are they unloading her?"

"They're taking boxes and such off and stacking them up on the dockside. There's about the biggest black man I ever did see with a club standing watch over them."

She had the right ship, that was clear. "That's Big Tom," I said. "He don't like black folks."

"Why not?" she said.

"I don't know," I said. "I guess it's because he wants white folks to favor him instead of other black folks."

"Well, he looks mighty scary to me," she said. "I wouldn't mess with him if I was you, Dan. Now come on. I got to get this fish back. You promised."

So I picked up the barrow handles and started off at a trot, with Nosy clipping along beside me, and we got back quick enough so that Nosy didn't get cursed out by the cook, only a couple of dirty looks.

Now at least I knew where the soldiers' notes was. They wouldn't be there for long, though. Captain Ivers wasn't going to leave the cargo sitting around on the dock, no matter who was standing guard over them. If he didn't find a buyer for them right away, he'd put them in a storehouse somewheres. I'd have to do something about them quick. But I didn't get much of a chance to think about it, because word came that I was to help out in the stables to work out my keep, and the stable boss kept me on the jump the rest of the morning.

But about the middle of the afternoon things slackened off a little, and I sat down on a bale of hay and gave it a little thought. The first thing that worried me was that if Mr. Fraunces or Mr. Fatherscreft knew what I had in mind, they'd probably stop me, or at least try to. I don't know why they was worried about me; as far as they was concerned, I was just another darky without no home. But they was worried about me, that was clear. Part of it had to do with Mr. Fatherscreft being a Quaker. And of course if Mr. Fraunces really was black, that would explain another part of it; but I didn't know if he was black, and anyway, being black didn't make Big Tom any nicer to his own kind.

No, it had mainly to do with my daddy. They respected my daddy, there wasn't any two ways about that. It was a funny thing, here he was drowned and all, and he was helping me more than he could if he was alive. And that was the reason I wasn't going to quit on those soldiers' notes. If I left Mum up there in Newfield to rot, I'd never be able to think about my daddy again as long as I lived without feeling terrible. A feeling like that would be worse than slavery. So I was going to take the chance. And that meant not letting on to Mr. Fraunces or Mr. Fatherscreft.

But who would I get to help? The only person I knew was Nosy, and she wasn't nothing but a child. But she wasn't stupid, neither. And I figured she'd help me, so as not to be left out.

I didn't have a chance to talk to her until suppertime, when we was on the ground out in the yard with our backs up against the shed wall, eating bowls of stew. "Now listen, Nosy," I said. "Are you game to help me out again? It's a mighty scary adventure."

"You bound to get into trouble, Dan."

"I'm already in enough trouble so's a little more won't matter very much. Tonight, after it gets dark, we're going back to the *Junius Brutus* and get my daddy's soldiers' notes. There's just one little thing you have to do. It ain't scary at all. I'll do all the scary parts."

"Mr. Fraunces, he'll kill me if I get into trouble."

"He ain't going to know about it. It's a secret between you and me. And afterward we'll be heroes."

Well, she was torn about it. I could see that. She wanted to go with me, that was for sure; but on the other side of it, she knew that she could get into a peck of trouble for helping me out. "You sure nobody's gonna know?"

"Sure as sunrise," I said. "You ain't going to say nothing, and I ain't going to say nothing, so how would anybody find out?"

I left it like that. We finished up our suppers, and she went back into the kitchen to help wash up the dishes. About an hour later she came out into the yard to pump some water. I came up to her. "Soon's it gets dark we'll go, Nosy. Bring your barrow."

I stayed out in the yard, mostly hanging around the shed where nobody would notice me. It came to be seven o'clock. The time went awful slow, but finally it was near full dark. I could see Nosy through the kitchen window, messing around with the plates. Finally she came out into the yard to pump up another bucket of water. I crossed over the yard. "Let's go," I said.

She looked at me like she was hoping I'd forgot about it. "I got to fill the water barrel."

"How long will that take?"

"What are we going to do, Dan?"

"I'll show you when we get there. Now swipe the oyster knife when you come."

"You're going to get in trouble, Dan."

"I don't care," I said. "Now finish up quick, so we can get going."

She didn't want to do it, I could see that, but she would. And about ten minutes later she came out of the kitchen drying her hands on her skirt. We got the barrow, loaded it up with hay, and hid the oyster knife in it. Then we slipped around the tavern as quiet as we could and set out along Broad Street. I was pretty nervous, all right. There was a lot of risk to it. But I didn't have any choice except to give up on the notes.

Even though it was night there was a few people going along the streets. The streetlights made their shadows loom up sudden on the walls of the houses, then shrink down again as they walked away from the light. There was plenty of live-stock, too, mostly lying down snoozing.

We came across Dock Street until we was just a block away from the waterfront. I stopped. "Nosy, which way's the brig?"

She pointed. "Up there."

We made a turn and worked our way along behind the waterfront for about fifteen minutes until I figured we was at about the right place. Then I told Nosy to wait, and I slipped forward sort of crouched over in the shadows of the buildings. In a moment I come to the corner. I pressed myself close against the building and eased my head around just a hair to get a look.

There were streetlights here, too, and lanterns hanging on some of the ships, so it was light enough to see a good distance. There was the street, and a mess of ships tied up to the docks every which ways, so that a lot of the bowsprits stuck out over the street like branches of trees. There was just a little breeze, making a kind of whispery noise in all those lines. The ships rocked a little, and I could hear loose lines slapping on the masts and them all creaking in different tones as if they was alive and complaining. There was two or three fires along the street, with sailors lounging around them, smoking, drinking rum, and talking to some women who was there. They looked mighty tough.

Down the street a little ways was the *Junius Brutus*. On the wharf in front of her was a stack of boxes and barrels. And sitting on one of the barrels, with his arms folded across his chest and his club across his lap, was Big Tom, his scar red as fire.

The stack of boxes and barrels was kind of pitiful. The storm had destroyed the largest part of the cargo. The deck cargo had gone overboard, and a lot of the stuff in the hold, like grain and

114

such had got ruined by the saltwater. I could see the linen chest, though, its shiny cherrywood gleaming in the streetlight. It was on top of a stack of other boxes tied round with cord. It wouldn't take Nosy more than ten seconds to cut the cord, grab the notes out, and stick them under the hay.

I pulled back and slipped down to where Nosy was standing with the barrow. My heart was going a mile a minute, and my hands was damp with sweat. "All right, Nosy," I said. "Here's what you got to do. There ain't nothing to it. You remember that big black fellow you saw this morning? Well, he's sitting out there on a barrel. Next to him there's a cherrywood chest with a cord around it. I want you to go out there with your barrow and just ease along aways. The minute he jumps off that barrel to chase after me, you cut that cord with the oyster knife, grab those notes out of the box, and stick them under the hay. Then you just ease off down the next street and head back to the tavern."

"What if he don't chase after you?"

"Don't worry about that none, Nosy. He will. You got it straight?"

"Dan, I'm scared."

"You ain't got nothing to be scared of. I'm the one he's going to be chasing."

"Dan, you're gonna be in a lot of trouble if he catches you."

"He ain't going to catch me, Nosy. Now you just do what I tell you. You're going to be a hero tomorrow."

She eased out onto Ferry Street, pushing the barrow in front of her. None of the sailors paid her no mind. She was just a little black girl pushing a barrow full of hay, and about as important as dirt. I figured Big Tom wouldn't even notice her. I waited until she was about twenty feet away from him. Then I took a deep breath to calm my nerves down and stepped out onto Ferry Street myself.

The main thing was to draw Big Tom as far down the street as I could. He wasn't going to have only trouble catching up with me once he got going, so it was important to get myself a good lead. I began to trot toward him, holding my head bent forward and turned away from him. I sure didn't want him to spot me until I was ready for it. I passed Nosy. She gave me a look, which she shouldn't have done because it might give it away that we were together. I didn't look at her but just sailed on by. Four steps farther and I was coming right up to Big Tom. I raised my head so he could see it and sort of gasped out, "Big Tom," as if it had taken me by surprise to come upon him, and then I began to run as fast as I'd ever run in my life.

"Arabus," he shouted. "Stop." His footsteps began to clunk on the cobblestones, and I went full tilt down Water Street. It wasn't easy going, for there was cargo standing everywhere in stacks and heaps and I had to keep dodging back and forth. But Big Tom had to dodge, too, and I had the advantage because I knew which way I was was going to dodge, and he didn't. By maneuvering right, I could keep stacks of things between him and me. Still, by the sound of his footsteps, I knew he was gaining on me.

When I'd gone about a hundred yards, I took a chance and swung my head around. Big Tom wasn't more than twenty feet behind me. His mouth was open and I could see all those busted teeth and the red scar clear as day. A cold shiver ran up my back. But behind him, in the distance, I could see Nosy and the barrow disappearing around the corner onto Ferry Street. I swung my head back around and swerved off the street onto the dockside. The ships were packed in close to each other, with hardly any space between. "Arabus," Big Tom shouted. He wasn't more'n ten feet behind me now.

I kept on running, looking for a gap between the ships. Then I saw on up ahead a space where a ship had gone out. I veered toward it. "Arabus," Big Tom shouted. Something slapped on my back, and I knew he'd made a grab for me and missed. I ran for the water. "Arabus." The hand hit my back again, and this time his fingers clutched at my collar. He jerked me back, and I twisted around. He had me. He loomed over me like a great black tower and swung his free hand back to lam me. I ducked forward, threw my hands up over my head, and jerked backward. My shirt slid up over my head, I pulled my arms free, tumbled back onto the dock, and rolled into the water. "Arabus," he shouted.

I sunk down and swum under water as long as I could, and then I burst up on top and looked back at the dock. He was standing there with my shirt in his hands. He was shouting and cursing, but there wasn't anything he could do about it, because he couldn't swim anymore than the rest of them. Suddenly he left off shouting and dashed away. I figured he was heading back to the brig to get the longboat and come after me.

But it was going to take him awhile to get started, because first he'd have to get one of the other men to guard the cargo, and then he'd have to lower the longboat into the water. I turned and began to swim along the harbor in the opposite direction. When I'd covered a couple of hundred yards, I swum in between two ships that was tied up there, hoisted myself up onto the dock, and broke for Fraunces Tavern.

Chapter Ten

We'd got the notes back. Nosy slept with them tucked down in her shirt. In the morning I took them up into the hayloft of the stable and hid them down in the hay way at the back of the loft, where the hay wasn't likely to be touched until the winter. I couldn't decide about telling Mr. Fraunces about getting them back. I'd probably want him to help me sell them, but I knew he was likely to be mighty sore about me and Nosy taking a chance like that.

But before I got a chance to think it over, Nosy came out to the stables where I was working and told me that I was supposed to go see the Quaker, Mr. Fatherscreft, in his room up there on the top floor of the tavern. I dropped my pitchfork, washed up a little bit, went on up, and knocked at his door. "Come in," he said.

I went in. Mr. Fatherscreft was lying in bed

still, but he'd got himself shaved, and he didn't look so pale as he had before. Mr. Fraunces was there, too, sitting on a chair by one of the little windows. I shut the door. They both looked at me. I didn't say anything. Then Mr. Fraunces said, "I hear you did something foolish last night, Arabus."

I went hot and prickly. "How'd you know that, sir?"

"You don't think Carrie would keep a good story like that to herself, do you?"

"Oh," I said. I never figured she'd go bragging about what we'd done, for fear of getting into trouble herself. I should have known better.

"Thou hast thy father's notes, then, Daniel?" Mr. Fatherscreft said.

"Yes, sir," I said. "I hid them out in the hayloft."

He gave a little cough. "I'd be glad to hold them for thee, Daniel," he said. "It might be safer that way."

I thought about it for a minute. "Yes, sir, I guess it would."

Then I noticed that Mr. Fraunces was looking at me kind of funny. "Dan, that was a foolish stunt you tried last night. You might have spent the rest of your life in the cane fields as a result of it."

"I know there was a risk, but I couldn't have gone off free myself and let Mum up in Connecticut to work for the Iverses for the rest of her life."

120

"It was brave, Daniel," Mr. Fatherscreft said.

"Oh, I wasn't a hero. I was scared to death the whole time."

Mr. Fatherscreft coughed a couple of times. He took a swallow of rum. Nobody said anything for a minute. Then he said, "Daniel, Mr. Fraunces and I have been talking about thee. Thou're clearly an intelligent and resourceful boy. I expect to go to Philadelphia to the convention shortly. Perhaps tomorrow. I'll need somebody to travel with me."

"Mr. Fatherscreft is only barely well enough to travel, Daniel," Mr. Fraunces said. "He'll need somebody to look after him. It'll get you away from New York, besides."

Well, there wasn't anything calculated to please me more. "Yes, sir," I said. "I'd sure be glad of the chance." But I didn't get a chance to say anything more, for just then there came a knock on the door. Mr. Fraunces opened it. The man who came in was tall and slim and dressed as fine as could be.

"William Few," he said, and shook Mr. Fraunces's hand. Then he went over to the bed and shook Mr. Fatherscreft's hand, too. "How are you feeling, Peter?"

"Better, I'm happy to say."

I slunk over to the wall to be out of the way.

"Able to travel, I hope?"

"Will there be reason for traveling?"

"I think we have hope of compromise, Peter. I've canvassed the Southerners here in Congress.

We'll vote with you to outlaw slavery in the North-west Territories, if the men at the convention will refrain from attempting to close the backlands south of the Ohio River to slavery, and if you'll give us a fugitive-slave provision in the new constitution."

I didn't know exactly who Mr. Few was or what he was talking about, but it had to do with the convention, that was pretty clear. Some way, he and Mr. Fatherscreft was bargaining out what would happen to us black people if a new constitution got written. It was sort of queer that it was all going to be decided by white folks, and us black folks wouldn't have no say in it at all. But we had to be thankful that at least there was some white people around like Mr. Fatherscreft who was on our side and would try to get the best bargain he could for us.

"What about prohibiting the further importation of slaves?" Mr. Fatherscreft said.

"We'll support a compromise that blocks any interference with the foreign slave trade for twenty years," Mr. Few said.

"And after that, William?"

"We wish the question of the further importation of Negroes to be left open after the twenty-year period. It can be taken up again then. Let the next generation decide whether Negroes shall or shall not be imported."

Mr. Fatherscreft didn't say nothing but lay in his bed, staring down at his hands. "My people were hoping for something better, William. We didn't expect that the new constitution would prohibit slavery now, but we were hoping that we could see that happening in the near future."

Mr. Few pursed his lips. "There's too much opposition. The big planters see the whole agricultural system as based on slavery. They can't bargain this away. They won't interfere if the Northern states decide to give up their own slaves, but the Southerners can't allow themselves to be put in a position where someday a group of new states will vote against them."

"In other words we're going to create a country with slave labor in the South and free labor in the north—a country divided from its first day."

It is the best compromise we can get, Peter."

Mr. Fatherscreft sighed. "And what about the fugitive-slave law?"

"We must have it. The more northern country that's free territory, the easier it'll be for southern blacks to run away. Why, with this compromise all they have to do is paddle across the Ohio River to get to free soil. Hundreds, maybe thousands, are running away every year as it is. We've got to protect our property. That's what a government is for, isn't it? And these black folks are our most valuable property. The Northerners will have to agree to help us recover the runaways."

Mr. Fatherscreft shook his head. "It's asking too much, William. It'll rankle those of us who are opposed to slavery to be forced to assist in returning fugitives to their owners."

Suddenly it struck me that they was talking about me. I was a fugitive slave. I'd run off, there was no question about that, even if I did mean to go back and pay Captain Ivers for myself. I was a fugitive slave, and if the constitution came out the way Mr. Few wanted it, why, Mr. Fatherscreft and Mr. Fraunces would be obliged by law to turn me back to Captain Ivers or risk going to jail themselves.

"I understand the feelings of your people, Peter. You know I lived many years among Quakers. But in the Congress, I represent the state of Georgia. And I have to tell you that in the South there's the fear that anti-slavery folks will encourage slaves to run away unless there are strong measures taken to prevent it."

"Isn't there any way around it, William?"

"I'm afraid not."

There it was. They'd bargained away the chance for thousands of black folks to escape, me included. The minute the constitution was agreed to, anybody who knew me would be bound by law to catch me and send me back to the Iverses in chains. Oh, it made me sad and sick to think of it. But there wasn't anything I could do about it. To them, I was just a fugitive slave and didn't matter more'n an ant matters to a dog. I didn't want to hear any more of it, either. They wasn't paying attention to me, so I opened the door real quiet, slipped out of the room, and went on down

124

the back stairs to the kitchen.

I tell you, I was pretty mixed up in my feelings. On the one hand, they'd bargained us blacks into slavery forever. On the other hand, if there was no bargain, maybe there'd be no new government and my soldiers' notes wouldn't be worth a penny.

I went back down to the stables, found the oil-cloth with the notes in it, and tucked it under my shirt. Then they gave me a rag and some water and sent me out front to wash the windows along the Broad Street side. After a while Mr. Fraunces and Mr. Few came down and got into a carriage and went off. Mr. Fraunces gave me a look as he passed by, but he didn't say nothing. Then around lunchtime Nosy came out with her barrow and headed off to the docks for fish.

Polishing windows was easy work, so I went slow and careful to make it last longer. And I was still working on the Broad Street side when Nosy came back with her barrow. I was glad to see her. When you got down to it, she was the best friend I had there—maybe the only one, too. She was all right, even if she was just a child, and nosy in the bargain. "Hey, Nosy," I said. "How about stealing me a roll when you're in the kitchen."

"You can't get yourself in enough trouble, you got to get me in some, too, Dan?"

"And get a nice big piece of cheese, too."

She stuck out her tongue at me, and I started to laugh. But then I stopped right quick, for coming along Broad Street about fifty feet behind Nosy was Captain Ivers and Big Tom. Quick as a flash I ducked into the front door, dashed through the dining room, and went on up the back stairs, but I knew they'd spotted me, for as I went through the door I heard Captain Ivers shout my name. I flew up the stairs, ran into Mr. Fatherscreft's room, slammed the door, and flung the bolt to.

"Daniel?" Mr. Fatherscreft said.

"It's them. Captain Ivers and Big Tom. They came to the tavern."

"Did they see thee?"

"Yes," I gasped out. My heart was pounding and my knees was shaking. "They'll be prowling around looking for me right this minute."

"Well. Now. What's to be done?"

"I don't know, sir. When are we supposed to leave for Philadelphia?"

"As soon as we can. We and the Southern interests have reached our compromise agreement. It's not what I had hoped for, but it's the best we can get. I must go immediately and bring the agreement to the delegates at the convention to act on. I would like to leave this evening." Suddenly he put his fist to his mouth and began a fit of coughing.

I waited until he calmed down some. "Sir, you ain't fit for traveling," I said.

"It doesn't matter," he said. He swallowed some rum. "I'm well enough."

"Maybe somebody else could take the message

126

for you."

"It has to come from me. I was the one empowered to negotiate for our side. They won't trust a stranger."

"I just wish you wasn't coughing so bad, sir."

"It's nothing. The rum helps. Now, dost thou suppose thy companions from the brig have left?"

I shook my head. "No, sir. If I know Captain Ivers, he'll be downstairs keeping a lookout for me. I'm worth a lot of money to him. He ain't going to let that go easy."

"Dost thou think thou can get away?"

"I sure have to try," I said. "They'll catch me sooner or later if I stay here." I was plenty scared.

"Yes," he said. "But your father was brave, and you'll be brave, too."

He sure seemed to know a lot about my daddy. "How did you get to meet him, sir?" I asked.

"Oh, that lawsuit thy father won was well known among those of us working against slavery."

"The one to get his freedom from Captain Ivers?"

"It was quite important to the Negroes' cause."

"I didn't know that," I said.

"Thy father enlisted in the army with the understanding that he would be set free at the end of his service."

"Why would Captain Ivers do that?"

"Oh, the captain wanted thy father to go as a substitute for him."

"So he wouldn't have to fight himself?"

It was a common practice during the war among those who could afford it to pay somebody to fight in their places. Or, as in this case, offer a Negro slave his freedom if he would go. I believe that some three hundred blacks from Connecticut alone fought in the Revolution. A great many of them went as substitutes, just as thy father did. Thy father's lawsuit was important in making sure that those who did were granted their freedom." He put his fist over his mouth and had another burst of coughing.

"Wouldn't you take a chance of getting killed if you went as somebody's substitute?" I said.

"Oh, yes. Many did. Thy father was lucky. He served with distinction through much of the war."

"Nearly the whole of it," I said. "He fought for six years. Once he helped General Washington to cross a stream."

Mr. Fatherscreft smiled. "I've heard that story. I believe thy father liked to tell it."

"I guess he was boasting a little," I said.

"Thy father was entitled to boast a little. I met him first when he was in jail. He wasn't frightened to fight for his rights." He coughed. "When Captain Ivers refused him his freedom, he left. Captain Ivers had him arrested and jailed for running away. I visited him in jail to comfort him. He wasn't in long, and he went on to win his case. Thy father was famous, for a time. He may well go down in history."

It certainly made me proud to hear that. Pretty

near anybody could have led General Washington's horse across a stream, if he had any brains at all. But for a black man to sue a white man, just like he was as good as anybody, why, that was a terrible daring thing to do. I don't know as I would have the nerve to do it. But my daddy, he wasn't scared of it, and he done it. Oh, that made me feel proud. "Was my daddy the first nig—" I stopped. I was blamed if I was going to say "nigger" anymore. "Was he the first Negro who did something like that?"

"Oh yes, Daniel. Some other Negroes had sued for their freedom before that, but thy father was the first to show that fighting in the war for our nation's independence should get him his freedom, too." He shook his head. "Well. We can talk about this some other time. We have other things to do."

"Yes, sir."

"The principal task right now is to get thee out of the tavern. If thou can manage to slip out, we can arrange to meet with the carriage later."

I was pretty worried about getting out. "Where would I meet you?"

"There's a church on Broadway near Wall Street, just a few blocks west and north. Make thy way there, and we'll send Carrie to tell thee where to join us."

It was an easy enough plan. The big question was where Captain Ivers and Big Tom were. There was a back stairs and a front stairs. They could each watch one. But I figured there was a chance that Captain Ivers would have business to do. He'd leave Big Tom to watch for me. But would he watch the back stairs or the front ones? The back, I decided: he'd figure that a nig—Negro would use the back stairs, not the front ones.

Quiet as I could, I slid the bolt on the door, and then I pulled the door open a crack and took a look out into the hall. There wasn't anybody there. I stepped out into the hall, shut the door behind me, and began to creep down the hall toward the front stairs. When I got to the top of the stairs, I pulled myself tight against the wall and eased my head around just a hair to get a look down them.

There wasn't anybody there, either: Feeling a lot easier, I let out a breath. I reckoned that if they'd been keeping a watch on me, they'd have stuck right there on the stairs. But they hadn't, so I began to go down the stairs a little quicker; the sooner I got out of the tavern, the better. I hit the bottom of the flight of stairs, and it was just then that Big Tom jumped out in front of me from somewheres, his eyes bulging and his teeth bared, and made a grab for me. Behind him was Captain Ivers.

I ducked and scrambled back up the stairs with Big Tom racing after me. At the top he made another grab for me, but I saw it coming and ducked away. Then I raced down the hall, into Mr. Fatherscreft's room, slammed the door, and bolted it. Outside, Big Tom banged on the door with his fist. "I've got you now, Arabus," he shouted. "You're trapped." He laughed a big roaring laugh.

Chapter Eleven

I dashed to the window and looked out. It was four stories straight down to the street. There wasn't any way I could get out there. In the hall I heard Captain Ivers shout, "If they won't open up, bust down the door, Tom." Big Tom wouldn't have any trouble doing that.

The only other way out of the room was the chimney. I jumped over to it, ducked my head down, and looked up. At the top I could see a patch of blue sky. The chimney looked like it was big enough to take me. "Mr. Fatherscreft," I said,

"I'll be waiting at the church." Then I ducked into the fireplace as another great crash came from the door. I reached my arms up over my head and felt around. In a couple of seconds I found some little cracks where the mortar had dropped out from between the bricks. I dug my fingers in and heaved myself up until I was a couple of feet off the ground. Then I drew my knees up to sort of jam myself in and reached up to get another handhold.

Just then there came a tremendous rip of splintering wood. I heard a scrambling and a tearing sound, and Big Tom and Captain Ivers piled into the room. "Where is he?" Captain Ivers shouted at Mr. Fatherscreft.

"There's nobody here, sir," Mr. Fatherscreft said.

I heard steps, and then the window squeaked open, and I reckoned that Big Tom was having a look to see if I could have got out that way. I dug my fingers in and heaved myself up again. The window squeaked closed, and the next thing I knew, Big Tom was looking up the chimney. I couldn't see his face too well for the dark, but his big head about filled the whole view. "Arabus," he shouted. "Come down." He reached up with his arm to grab at my legs, but I pulled my knees up quick and he couldn't catch me. I took another handhold and pulled myself farther up.

Big Tom disappeared, but in a minute he was back down there at the bottom of the chimney again. This time he had a sharp stick which had splintered out of the door when he'd busted it. He shoved it up the chimney like a sword. It caught me in the leg, a good sharp jab. "Come down," he roared. But I pulled myself up again, and then I felt above the top edge of the chimney, and I pulled myself up and out.

The tavern had a mansard roof, a flat center part with the sides sloping away from it. There was a low rail fence around the flat part, so's you could walk around up there without risk of falling off. A trap door leading down to the hall below was at one end. I figured in about a minute Big Tom would be coming up it.

I dashed toward the back and looked down. The roof sloped off for about fifteen feet. Then it dropped straight down two stories to the roof of one of the little sheds out back. If I could somehow get down onto that shed roof, it would be easy enough to drop to the ground from there. But to do that, first I'd have to slide down those steep, slippery slates for fifteen feet and then find some way to climb down the outside of the tavern for two stories to the shed roof.

I took another look around. There wasn't any other way out. It was either slide down that roof and risk falling off, or stay there and get caught by Big Tom. I looked down the sloping roof again. There was a wooden rain gutter running along the bottom edge. I was pretty sure that it

133

would support my weight. It had to be strong enough to hold a lot of snow and ice in the wintertime. I figured I could probably grab onto it when I slid down and keep myself from going all the way over the edge. There was certain to be a downspout running to the cistern somewheres, probably at the corner of the building.

Just then I heard a thump underneath the trap door. I couldn't wait any longer: I had to make up my mind. Oh, my, that roof looked steep, and I knew that those slates would be slippery as ice. There was another thump, and the trap door squeaked open. I swiveled around to look. Big Tom's head was poking out. I swung my leg over the rail fence, sat down on the slates, let go of the railing, and started to slide down the roof. I tried to sort of grab at the slats as I went along, to slow myself down, but there wasn't anything really to grab on to, and I began to pick up speed. The gutter came rising up to me. I jammed my feet out to catch in it, but they didn't catch, and I started to ride right over the edge of the roof. I grabbed with my hands, and the next thing I knew I was dangling by my arms from the gutter, two stories up above the little shed roof.

Above me I heard Tom's roaring laugh. "You're a fool, Arabus," he shouted. "You're going to kill yourself sure."

I twisted my head back to look up, but from that angle I couldn't see anything but the underside of the gutter and the sky. My hands was beginning to hurt already. I thought about just letting go and dropping. I figured I could probably fall two stories, which wasn't more'n about twenty feet, without getting hurt too bad. But there was always the chance that I'd break a leg, or plunge through the shed roof, or even maybe just sprain an ankle. If I couldn't run, he'd catch me in a minute.

I twisted my head to look sideways. There was a downspout, just as I'd figured, running down the corner of the building. I began to move along the gutter, first swinging my body to one side and then reaching out with my hand to get a fresh grip. Above me I heard Big Tom running, and then the trap door slamming, and I knew he was racing down the stairs to catch me when I hit the ground.

I reached the downspout. It was about four inches thick. I grabbed it with both hands and just let myself slide down as fast as I dared. My hands burned, but I knew I was in for a lot worse than that if Tom caught me. I hit the shed roof, dashed to the edge, and jumped down onto the ground. I tumbled when I hit, but I was up in a flash and racing the back way out of the tavern yard onto Broad Street. I ran as hard as I could for four or five blocks till I came to City Hall and turned west. In a minute I was inside the church, hunched over in a pew like I'd come in to say my prayers.

135

I sat there for the rest of the afternoon, not daring even to look around in a case Big Tom or Captain Ivers came prowling around. Finally, around suppertime Nosy came for me. She tapped me on the arm, and we went out of the church into the street. "Where you been?" she said. "You look mighty scuffed up."

"Well, Nosy, all I did was climb up the chimney, slide down the roof, and shinny down the drainpipe. That wouldn't be likely to scuff anybody up, would it?"

"I'll bet you was scared."

"Scared? Not me, Nosy. Who'd be scared of being chased up a chimney and sliding down a roof four stories up?"

"I'll bet you were," she said.

"Nothing like it," I said. "Now stop asking questions and tell me where the carriage is."

It was in the next street. We trotted around there. It was an ordinary black carriage, with Mr. Fatherscreft's chests tied on top near the driver and two seats inside facing each other that was big enough for three each. Except that there wasn't anybody inside but Mr. Fatherscreft and Mr. Fraunces.

"Jump in, Daniel," Mr. Fraunces said. I hopped in. Mr. Fatherscreft was wrapped up in a blanket, looking pale and sweaty. He wasn't in no shape to travel, I could tell that right away. "Daniel, stay down on the floor until you're clear of the city." I dropped to the floor and crouched there. "Now,

136

Daniel, bear it in mind that Mr. Fatherscreft is not well. You're to keep things as quiet and easy for him as you can. Understand?"

"Yes, sir," I said. Then he got out of the carriage and looked up at the driver. "All right," he said.

I poked my head up just a little to get a look at Nosy. I guess I liked her. I wished I had a chance to say good-bye and maybe give her a little hug, too. But I couldn't risk getting out of the carriage, where somebody might spot me. All I could do was give her a wave, and then I dropped down out of sight again. The carriage began to move, the wheels creaking and rumbling on the street. Still I felt sorry to leave Nosy. I might never see her again. So I raised up and took a look out of the back window. Nosy and Mr. Fraunces were standing there, watching us go. I wondered if I'd ever see them again in my life.

I gave them another wave, and then I saw, standing back aways down the street, Big Tom. staring right at me. I dropped to the floor in a flash, but I knew it wasn't any use: he'd seen me. My heart sank. I knew what had happened. He'd hung around the tavern after I escaped, waiting for me to come back. When he saw Mr. Fatherscreft get into the carriage, he'd got suspicious and followed along. I was lucky in one thing, though. If it had been Captain Ivers, he'd have come right over and demanded me back as a runaway. But Big Tom was black and couldn't come around and start giving orders to white folks.

He would go after Captain Ivers, though, I figured; or else follow us to see where we went, and then get him, one way or the other. I began to pray that we'd get across the North River first. I lay on the floor, watching the tops of the houses go along, my heart beating, and just hoping and praying I'd make it safe across the river before Captain Ivers caught up to us. Then I began to smell harbor smells. "The ferry," Mr. Fatherscreft said.

I took a chance and raised my head. I didn't see Big Tom anywheres. The ferry was loading, and a crowd of people and wagons was waiting their turn to go on. It took us ten minutes before we were on, and another five minutes to cast off. Oh, my heart was racing like a scared horse, but we pulled away from shore, and half an hour later we landed at Paulus Hook on the New Jersey shore. But I didn't feel really safe until we'd got off the ferry and turned into Smith's Tavern, just a little ways from the ferry. Once we was up in our room and I got Mr. Fatherscreft a dram of rum and tucked him in bed, I let go a big sigh. Finally I was safe from Big Tom and Captain Ivers. But I was pretty sure they wouldn't give up on me. The most usual thing would be to have a handbill describing me printed and hung up in taverns and on walls. Probably they'd offer a reward for me, too. It scared me to think about that. But for now, anyway, I was safe.

138

Mr. Fatherscreft woke up a couple of times in the night with a coughing fit. I gave him a little rum each time, and in the end he slept pretty good. In the morning he seemed a little better. We got started just after daybreak. It was a good two days' trip to Philadelphia.

Between having got away from Captain Ivers and Mr. Fatherscreft seeming a little better, I was feeling pretty cheerful as we set out from Smith's Tavern for Bergentown. I'd never been anywheres in a carriage before. It wasn't the custom for black folks to ride in a style like that. Oh, I felt pretty grand riding along like that and taking in the view.

It was pretty interesting to see a foreign place like New Jersey. It was all different. They didn't have many wooden clapboard or shingle houses the way we did in Connecticut. In New Jersey they was mostly of stone, with piazzas across the front. Nor did I see so many oxen as I was accustomed to. The wagons was mostly drawn by horses, two or three abreast.

The land was flatter, too. At one place we went through a long marsh, four or five miles, I reckoned. We traveled through it on a narrow stone causeway just about wide enough for one carriage. There was breaks in the causeway, where we went over bridges or took ferries for a stretch. And after the marsh there was more ferries to take us across the Hackensack River and the Second River.

We came to a little village called Newark about eight o'clock in the morning and stopped at Pell's Tavern for breakfast. I reckoned I'd bring Mr. Fatherscreft his breakfast out to the carriage, but he said no, he was feeling better, he'd come into the inn. We had porridge, bread, and cheese— two shillings, six pence.

The breakfast put Mr. Fatherscreft in a talkative mood. "Daniel, thou art very lucky. Thou art privileged to take part in a great event."

"A great event, sir?"

"Oh, yes. If the convention can agree to a constitution, thou will be witness to the founding of a new nation. It has never happened this way before."

"There was never a new nation started before?"

Mr. Fatherscreft laughed a bit until he started to cough. "Of course there have been new nations. But always in the past they've come out of war or conquest. Never before have nations come together to settle for themselves what manner of government they shall have. For really, Daniel, each of the united states has been acting like an independent little country in most ways. But if we can compromise our differences between large states and small ones, between farmers and merchants, and especially between states dependent on slaves and those with few of them, Daniel, we will have done what has never been done before. We will have peaceably combined twelve or thirteen little republics into one great one."

Well, I didn't know much about history, so I reckoned he was right. "Sir, suppose they can't get together on it. I mean, suppose they can't agree about whether the big states should have more votes, or whether there ought to be slavery."

"Oh yes, Daniel, we're a long way from agreement yet. Some days I've been very doubtful of it all. But today I'm optimistic. We'll have our compromise on slavery, at least. It may not be what thou and I want, but it at least indicates that men of goodwill can find solutions to difficult problems."

It didn't seem like much of a solution to me, being as I was likely to stay a slave for the rest of my life. I didn't want to say so, though, so I switched the subject. "But if they agree, and get a constitution, then my daddy's soldiers' notes will be worth the whole six hundred dollars?"

Mr. Fatherscreft thought about that for a minute. "Not certainly, Daniel. And perhaps not right away. But there are men in the convention who own notes, too; and a good deal more than six hundred dollars, in many cases. I'll wager that they'd be worth something substantial within a year or so."

"So the best chance for me and Mum to be free is for the convention to agree to a constitution joining all the states into a new nation."

"No doubt of it, Daniel. What the convention

141

does over the next few weeks will touch thee deeply, as it will touch all of us."

When he put it that way, it seemed clear enough that I ought to be pushing for the new constitution as hard as I could. But there was another side to it. For according to the compromise Mr. Fatherscreft was carrying down to Philadelphia, the new country would have slavery in the South and a fugitive-slave law that said anybody who knew I was a runaway had to turn me in. And sooner or later I'd get caught, sure. Captain Ivers was bound to put out a reward for me. He was sure to be having handbills about me made already. That's what they always did. Somebody was certain to turn me in for the reward and feel he was doing the right thing, too.

Ot, it was a puzzle. On the one side of it, if the convention agreed, and we got a constitution, I'd have the soldiers' notes to buy me and Mum free. But on the other side of it, as soon as the constitution was signed, I was likely to be captured and turned back to Captain Ivers. The first thing he'd do would be to take those notes away from me and sell me South. And that would be the end of me forever.

And that's when something else came to me: why was I helping Mr. Fatherscreft bring a message down to Philadelphia that could put me into the cane fields for the rest of my life?

142

Chapter Twelve

Talking about this seemed to give Mr. Fatherscreft the idea that we shouldn't waste time, so we finished up breakfast quickly and started off again. We figured on reaching Trenton by nightfall and then crossing the Delaware River into Philadelphia the next day. Trenton was where my daddy had fought, and I wanted to see it.

We went along through some little places called Spanktown and Bonhamtown. There was beautiful farms along through here, especially orchards, with about every kind of fruit tree you could think of. I didn't know the names of them all, but Mr. Fatherscreft did, and he told them to me. About one o'clock in the afternoon we came into New Brunswick, a pretty big place on the Raritan River. There were lots of fancy houses here, mostly brick or stone.

We pulled through town and up to the ferry landing on the Raritan. There was lots of little boats out in the river going up and down. On a hill in the middle of town was a great brick building. Mr. Fatherscreft said it had been used for a barracks during the Revolution. I wondered if my daddy stayed there. While we were waiting for the ferry, we stopped at a little inn called The Lion and ate some pork and beans. Then we crossed the Raritan on the ferry and headed for Princeton, seventeen miles farther south. We got there at ten at night. I could see that Mr. Fatherscreft was pretty tired from the travelling. It wasn't doing him any good. His cough was worse, and I had to sort of help him along from place to place. We ate supper and went right to bed.

Mr. Fatherscreft woke up coughing three or four times in the night. I went downstairs for some rum, but there wasn't anybody around. The place was dark and shut up tight. I found a pitcher of beer somebody had left and brought that up to Mr. Fatherscreft, but it wasn't the same. "Daniel," he said in his weak voice, "I must rely on thee for everything now."

"You ain't that bad off, Mr. Fatherscreft," I said to cheer him up. "Once we get to Philadelphia, you can get a good long rest."

He reached out of bed, took my hand, and gave it a little squeeze. "Daniel, thou art a good lad. Don't ever let anybody tell thee otherwise. Take

144

pride in thyself."

"Yes, sir," I said. "I will." I meant it, too. My daddy, he was good as any white man, and I was determined that I would be, too.

In the morning I told Mr. Fatherscreft that we ought to go a little slower and maybe take a good long rest at noontime, so's he wouldn't get so tired out. He wouldn't hear of it. He was coughing pretty bad when we started off for Trenton, where we'd cross the Delaware River to Pennsylvania. But he was all fired up to get to Philadelphia as soon as we could. He'd rest when we got there, he said. I knew what he was thinking. He was thinking that he was bound to die soon, and he wanted to get to Philadelphia with his message before he went.

So he sat up, and coughed and dozed between times, and I tried to enjoy the view out the window. It was rich country; there was rye and oats and barley growing in the fields, and here and there they were reaping the wheat and tying it up in shocks in the fields to dry. But worrying about Mr. Fatherscreft maybe dying took most of the fun out of looking at the scenery, so after a while I lay down on my seat and tried to doze, too.

By the end of the afternoon Mr. Fatherscreft wasn't so much coughing as just lying back gasping for breath. He was hot and sweaty, too. We still had three or four miles into Trenton. Twice I had the driver stop by streams to get Mr. Fatherscreft some cold water. It didn't seem to help much. He went on gasping.

Finally, as the sun was going down, we came into Trenton. There was a little creek through it, and a big stone mill. We didn't stop but went right on through the town and out the other side to the ferry crossing on the Delaware. There was a tavern at the ferry landing called Vandergrift's. We pulled in here, and I hauled Mr. Fatherscreft out of the coach and into the tavern.

He had got so weak from coughing that I had to sort of drape him over my shoulders to get him up to his room. I propped him up in bed to ease his coughing, and wrapped him up good in a blanket. His face was soaked in sweat, and every once in a while he gave a big shiver. "Daniel," he said in a voice so low I could hardly hear it, "we can be In Philadelphia tomorrow if we get an early start. I must live that long. I must."

"Don't worry, Mr. Fatherscreft, you ain't going to die. I'll see to that. You just rest now and don't do ro more talking. I'm going to get you some rum."

I got a full bottle so I'd have enough for the night. He had trouble swallowing it, but I got some in him, and he dozed off. I was feeling pretty nervous and shaky, so I had a dram of it myself and lay down on the floor to sleep.

But Mr. Fatherscreft's breathing was coming so hard I couldn't doze off. It was loud and raspy as somebody sharpening a saw with a file. After a bit I got up and stood looking out the window at

146

the Delaware River. It was three-quarters of a mile wide, as near as I could judge. The sun was going down in the west, laying great patches of red on the water. A ferry was coming across, loaded down with two or three wagons. Every little while a rider would come down the road to the tavern, tie up his horse, and come in for his dinner. It was a pretty sight, but I couldn't take pleasure in it for the rasping of Mr. Fatherscreft's breath behind me.

Finally the sun went down, and I lit a candle and had a look at Mr. Fatherscreft. His face was wet, as if somebody'd flung a bucket of water on him, and his hands was outside of the blanket, sort of picking and clutching at it, as if he was trying to hang on to something. I wondered if I ought to wipe his face off for him. I didn't want to wake him up, but I thought maybe he'd rest easier for it. So I set down the candle on the chair near the bed and took out my handkerchief. I guess it was the light shining in his eyes that done it, for before I touched him he gave a sudden jerk and sat half up, his eyes big as eggs staring out into the room. Then he blinked and fell back and lay there gasping.

"Daniel," he said in the low, hoarse voice, looking straight ahead. "I'm dying. Wipe my face."

I did it. "You ain't dying yet, sir. We'll make Philadelphia. Here, take some more rum."

"No, no, it's too late for rum," he said. "I'm dying, Daniel. It's up to you now; I've gone as far as I can go." Slowly he turned his head over to look at me. "Daniel, you say you know William Samuel Johnson." His voice was weak and low.

"Yes sir," I said, feeling pretty shaky. "I seen him around Stratford since I was born. My daddy worked for him sometimes. He said he'd help us after my daddy got drowned."

"You must find him. You must give him the message. Only him. Do you understand? To nobody else." He stared into my eyes hard.

"Yes sir," I said.

He took his hands off the blanket and snatched at my wrist. "Only to Johnson, Daniel, do you hear?" he said, all whispery, still staring into my face.

"Yes sir. I won't tell anybody else."

"Give me your word," he said, his eyes wide in the middle of that pale, wet face.

"Yes, sir, you have my word on it." I took the handkerchief and wiped his face dry.

"Daniel, tell Johnson that Congress will bar slavery north of the Ohio River, with nothing said about the South, new states or old. Tell him that if they give us this, we must accept a fugitive-slave law and leave the matter of slave importation till later."

His voice was so low and whispery now that I could hardly hear it, and I had to bend close over him to make out his words. "Yes, sir," I said.

148

"There's to be no slavery north of the Ohio River, but you won't make claim about the South."

He turned his face away from me. "And they can have their godless fugitive-slave law," he whispered. "They can have their slave law."

"Yes, sir," I said low. "They can have their fugitive-slave law."

And so it was going to be me was to carry the fugitive-slave law down to Philadelphia. It gave me a mighty queer feeling. But I didn't have time to think about it then, for Mr. Fatherscreft gave a big gasp, his breath stopped, and his body braced up into an arch and quivered there. I couldn't think of nothing to do but give him a shake. He stopped quivering, sucked in some air, and lay back down. "I'll get a doctor," I said. I raced out of the room and down the stairs into the taproom. It was filled with people at long benches eating and drinking and talking and laughing.

The tavern keeper was standing by the door, talking to a man who had just come in. The man was carrying some handbills and a hammer. I slipped across the room and touched the tavern keeper on the sleeve. "Sir, I need a doctor."

The tavern keeper swiveled around and gave me a hard look. "What do you mean interrupting, boy? Can't you see I'm talking."

"Sir, my master's dying," I said. "He needs a doctor."

"Dying?"

"Yes sir. He can't get his breath."

The other man gave the hammer a quick shake: "Where'll I put the handbill, then?" he asked.

The tavern keeper pointed toward the stairs: "Over there, by the stairs," he said.

"Sir, he's dying," I said.

"That's the old Quaker?"

"Yes, sir."

"It don't sound to me like a doctor'll be much use."

"Please, sir."

"I'll see what I can do."

"Thank you," I said. Then I turned away and slipped back to the stairs. The man with the hammer was standing at the foot of them, nailing the poster to the wall. I gave it a quick look. It said:

£10 REWARD
RUNAWAY SLAVE, AGE FOURTEEN, NAMED
DANIEL ARABUS. TRAVELING IN COMPANY
OF ELDERLY QUAKER. 5'6: OF MEDIUM
DARK COMPLEXION—

I didn't want to read anymore but took off up the stairs.

Chapter Thirteen

I slipped up the stairs as quick and quiet as I
could, got into our room, and threw the bolt. Then
I looked at Mr. Fatherscreft. He was lying where
I had left him. His eyes were open and he was
staring up at the ceiling. His face had gone gray
under the sweat. He wasn't breathing anymore. I
slipped across the room and touched him. His skin
was cold and clammy, and I knew he was dead.

Oh, he was an old man and sick, and bound to
die soon anyway. But still I felt awful bad. He'd
wanted to get to Philadelphia so much and now
he never would. I felt like I'd let him down. I'd
promised Mr. Fraunces that I'd take care of him,
and I hadn't done it. Oh, I knew it wasn't really
my fault, there wasn't any way I could have kept

him alive. But I wished I could have.

Still, it was making me feel kind of spooky being alone with a dead man, and that handbill downstairs. I decided the best thing for me to do was just leave. There wasn't anything more I could do for him. Anyway, the important thing was to get to Philadelphia with the message for William Samuel Johnson.

I didn't want to take a chance on going out through the tavern with that handbill hanging there. I went to the window and looked out. It was full night, but there was plenty of stars. There was light coming out of the tavern windows, too, and some lanterns down by the ferry landing. A wagon road ran down a hundred yards from the tavern to the ferry. On either side there was open fields, and along the river, a thin row of trees. The river was flowing so quiet that I could see starlight shining silver on it.

I opened up Mr. Fatherscreft's trunk and took out my soldiers' notes. Then I slipped open the window. I looked back at Mr. Fatherscreft. He was still staring up at the ceiling. I didn't want to touch him again, but I knew what was right, so I went over and closed his eyes for him. Then I slung myself over the windowsill, dropped out onto the ground, and began to trot along down toward the ferry.

On both sides of me there was open fields with split-rail fences. I veered off toward the left,

152

vaulted over the fence, and headed out across the field. The moon wasn't up yet, but there was enough starlight so anybody who was looking could see me running out there. I kept on going, fast as I could, toward the line of trees along the river, where I would be more in shadow. In a moment I was by the river. I didn't know exactly where I was, but the one thing I knew was that the Delaware River wound down to Philadelphia. All I had to do was follow it along.

But that was risky. There were handbills up for me. A black boy traveling by himself was bound to look suspicious, anyway. All anyone had to do was begin to ask me a few questions about who I was and where I was going, and I'd be done for.

Working my way along the riverbank was going to be slow, too. I had about thirty miles to go. It would take me more than a day, which meant I'd be traveling by day a good deal of the time. I looked at the river. It was about three-quarters of a mile wide and moving pretty swift. In a boat I could make pretty good time. The idea of stealing a boat was scary, though. If I got caught I'd be in a peck of trouble, all right.

But one way or another I had to start moving, so I began walking along downstream as fast as I could through the treeline. It was slow work. There were roots and stumps sticking up in the dark ground where I couldn't see them, and the bank was muddy and slippery. If I traveled only at night it'd take me two or three days to reach

Philadelphia. But there wasn't anything to do but keep on plugging away.

By the time the sky began to lighten in the east, I figured I'd covered maybe five miles. The dark turned to gray, and then I saw through the trees the pinkish glow of the sun working its way toward the horizon. And just about the same time I spotted the cabin on the riverbank with the little rowboat tied up to a tree in front of it.

I knew I had to steal it. Going along the way I was would take too long to get into Philadelphia. Besides, I was tired and sore from stumbling along the bank. I was scared to steal the boat. But there wasn't any way around it.

Then something came to me: why was I going to Philadelphia at all? Did I really want to carry a message to the convention that would put through the fugitive-slave law? For there I was, a fugitive slave myself, with posters up about me and people on my track. What difference would it make for the government to pay off the soldiers' notes if I was sold off to the West Indies first. Captain Ivers was on my trail. Big Tom had seen me going off with Mr. Fatherscreft in the coach. Probably Captain Ivers asked a few questions around Fraunces Tavern, and he'd be able to find out where Mr. Fatherscreft was headed. Then he'd come after me. On the road to Philadelphia an old Quaker traveling with a black boy wouldn't be hard to track.

There was a good chance that by the time I got to Philadelphia, those handbills would be up all around. The first time I showed my nose anywhere, I'd be nabbed quick as you could say it.

That made another good reason for not going to Philadelphia. When I looked around all sides of it, the only thing that made sense for me was to strike out west to the new lands that was opening up in Pennsylvania across the Allegheny Mountains. I knew how to get there, too, for Mr. Fatherscreft had told me that the Delaware flowed out of the new lands through a deep cut in the mountains on its way to Philadelphia. All I had to do was follow it upstream, and in a few days I'd be out on the frontier where nobody was likely to ask a lot of questions. If I could get anything at all for my soldiers' notes, maybe I could buy myself a little homestead, and if I had any luck, in a few years save up enough to buy Mum her freedom.

There was only one thing wrong with that idea, which was that I'd promised Mr. Fatherscreft I'd carry the message to Mr. Samuel Johnson. How could I go back on a promise to a dying man? Mr. Fatherscreft had been good to me, and he was trying to do the best he could for black people. Oh, it was a terrible problem. Stealing the boat and going on into Philadelphia was a sure-fire way to get myself in a mess—put back in slavery and get a beating and maybe put in jail, too. But how

155

could I go back on a promise like that? I stood there thinking about it. The minutes went by and I went on thinking about it. And then finally I told myself not to bother thinking about it anymore, there wasn't any way I could get around a promise to a dying man—a man who knew my father.

I slipped across to the cabin and had a look in the window. There was a man in there lying on a litt'e cornhusk mattress, sound asleep. I ducked back and slid down the bank to the rowboat. The oars were in it. Quickly I untied the rope from the tree. Then I eased out into the water, climbed in, and lay flat on the bottom, letting it drift downstream. I stayed that way with my head down for ten minutes. Then I figured I was far enough downstream to be out of sight of the cabin, and I sat up and began rowing.

What was going to happen to me now? It would be a sad thing for Mum to have me sold off to the West Indies. Then she'd be all alone, no husband, no son, no friends: just her working away for the rest of her life for the Iverses.

I wondered what she was doing just then. Was she thinking about me, the same as I was thinking about her? By this time she'd have learned about the shipwreck and Birdsey and all. Some Connecticut captain who'd been in New York was bound to have brought home the news. Did she know that Captain Ivers was planning to sell me off to the West Indies? Would Mrs. Ivers have told her that? I didn't know; but I knew she'd be worried about me, worried that I'd drowned or get hurt.

What would happen to her if I got caught? The only hope we had was in the soldiers' notes. And I didn't even know if they'd ever be worth anything. So I decided to stop thinking about it, and I sat in the boat, drifting along and looking at the sights.

Around the middle of the morning there began to be a road alongside the riverbank, and some houses and then people coming along the road on foot or horseback. I went drifting on, and a couple of hours later I came into Philadelphia harbor.

Chapter Fourteen

It was a pretty sight, with ships everywhere and a forest of masts and bowsprits sticking out over the harbor street. It was just as busy as New York harbor—men everywhere, loading ships from wagons and loading wagons from ships, or just lounging around; stacks of casks and boxes and piles of hay and barrels; small boats filled with fruit and vegetables tied to the wharves. There was a pretty good number of blacks around, too. One old fellow was sitting there smoking a pipe and playing queer tunes on a kind of fiddle made of gourds.

I didn't want to go drifting around the harbor in a stolen boat any longer that I had to, so I pulled up to the first dock I came to, tied up, and

158

climbed out, trying not to look nervous. I walked along the wharves a good way so as to be away from the boat I'd stolen, in case somebody came along and recognized it. Then I leaned up against a wall and waited until a black person came along and asked him how to get to the State House. It wasn't hard to get to, he said, and told me the way. In about twenty minutes I was standing in front of it, feeling pretty nervous.

I tell you, it was a fine great place, all brick, with lots of big windows sparkling in the sun, and carvings and patterns in the moldings around the door. There were gravel walks along the front and some little elm trees they'd just planted. And that wasn't all of it, either. On each side there was stone and brick buildings near as large as the State House. One of them was a prison, I could see that right away. Some of the prisoners was standing by the bars hollering out into the street. A few of them had got long poles, which they tied their caps to and stuck through the bars into the street so people could put pennies in the caps if they were feeling kind and had a mind to do it. And if nobody put anything in a cap, why the man who owned it would set up the most terrible cursing you ever heard. As I stood there watching the prisoners, it came to me that if Captain Ivers caught me, I might end up there, too.

But it was too late to worry about that. There was stone arches on either side between the State House and the other buildings. The arches opened onto a mall which ran out to the back. I walked through one of the arches. Just past it there was a door. I walked up the steps and opened it. I was mighty scared to go into a place of such importance, me being low as dirt, and my hand shook on the knob. But I knew I had to do it, so I went on in.

I was in a big hall. There was people in fancy clothes walking around and talking to each other. Some of them was delegates to the convention, I reckoned, and was bound to be famous, but I couldn't tell which.

Just inside the door there stood a soldier in blue, with a sword on one side of his belt and a pistol on the other. He put his arm out. "Hold up there, you," he said. "Deliveries around to the rear."

My knees was shaking. "I have a message for somebody, sir."

"All right. Give it to me."

"It ain't written out, sir. It's in my head."

He stared at me. "I don't believe it. Nobody'd give a nigger a message in his head. No nigger could ever get anything like that staight."

It made me mad, him saying that after all the trouble I'd been through to get there. "It's important," I said.

"Sure," he said. "They always are."

I was getting madder and madder. "It's for Mr. William Samuel Johnson."

"Sure," he said. "And I'm the Queen of May.

Now run along before I lock you up."

I could feel tears coming up behind my eyes, I was so mad. "I have to see him. I'm not lying, it's important." Just then I realized that a very fancy dressed man no bigger than me was staring at me.

"Guard," the man said, "please remove the nigger from the doorway so a gentleman can pass through."

The guard grabbed me by the arm and jerked me away. "I'm sorry, Mr. Hamilton," he said. "He's been trying to tell me that he has a message for Mr. William Samuel Johnson."

"No doubt," Mr. Hamilton said. I knew right away who it was: Mr. Alexander Hamilton, one of the most famous of all the men at the convention. He started to go for the door. I was scared to death, but I knew I had to do something. "Sir," I said. "I ain't lying. It's important."

Mr. Hamilton snapped his head around. "Guard, would you please keep this nigger away from me."

The guard grabbed for my arm and jerked me back hard, away from Mr. Hamilton. "I ain't lying," I cried out. "It's for Mr. Johnson from Mr. Fatherscreft."

Hamilton was halfway out the door, but he stopped dead and spun around. "Fatherscreft? Where is he? He was due here yesterday."

"He's dead, sir. He died of the cough last night at Trenton. He was mighty sick."

"Dead? Fatherscreft is dead?" He was speaking

161

in a loud voice, and I noticed that some of the other men in the hall had turned to look at us.

"Yes sir."

"And he gave you a message for us?"

"For Mr. Johnson, sir."

"All right. Give it to me."

Two or three other men had walked over to us and were standing there, listening. "I can't tell it to anybody but Mr. Johnson."

"What?" Mr. Hamilton shouted. "Why, I'll wring your neck, you impudent little wretch." He snatched at my shirt front. "Now tell me."

My mouth was bone dry and I could hardly talk, but scared as I was of Mr. Hamilton, I was more scared of going back on a promise to a dying man and being haunted all the rest of my life. "I can't, sir," I said. "I promised Mr. Fatherscreft. I can't go back on my promise."

He let go of my shirt. "What's your name, boy?"

"Daniel Arabus," I said.

"Arabus?"

Now one of the other men who had been standing by pushed forward. "What's all the commotion, Hamilton?"

"This darky says he has a message from Fatherscreft, General."

"What is your name, boy?"

I was scared before; now I was about ready to drop down onto the floor in a dead faint, for it was General Washington. I'd seen his picture

162

hanging in Fraunces Tavern. It was him, sure enough. "Arabus, sir," I sort of gasped out. "My daddy fought with you."

"He did, did he? Maybe I remember. Was it at Trenton? Where's he now?"

"He drowned, sir. He went out in the *Katey Lee* this spring and never came back. He helped you across a stream once. He held your horse."

General Washington smiled, and some of the others laughed. "I don't remember that. I remember the fighting at Trenton."

When he said that, the picture of my daddy came into my mind. I saw him standing there brave and strong, looking down at me, and I began to feel braver and stronger myself.

Mr. Hamilton turned to General Washington. "He has a message for Dr. Johnson. It's obviously word of the negotiations on the slavery issue. He says Fatherscreft is dead, and he won't tell anybody but Johnson. We'll have to wring it out of him."

"There's no need of that, Mr. Hamilton," General Washington said. "I won't ask the boy to go back on a deathbed promise. Dr. Johnson is in the writing room with one of his constituents." He took my arm. "We'll go see him, shall we, Arabus?"

We marched on with General Washington on one side of me and Mr. Hamilton on the other, and some of the other men coming along behind. Oh, I was scared half to death to be with such famous men. We crossed the hall and then turned

163

into a little room filled with fancy furniture—big captain's chairs, a lot of tables, and two fireplaces. I looked around, and that's when I got the most awful shock. Dr. Johnson was sitting at one of the tables with some papers in front of him. Sitting opposite him was Captain Ivers.

The minute Captain Ivers saw me he jumped to his feet. "Arabus," he shouted. Then he looked at General Washington, sort of confused.

Dr. Johnson stood up, too. "Your runaway slave seems to have run back to you, Captain," he said.

"He has a message from Peter Fatherscreft," General Washington said. "He won't give it to anybody but you. Johnson."

"Fatherscreft? At last. Where is the old soul?"

"He's dead, sir. He died last night at Trenton."

"Dead?"

"Yes, sir," I said. "He was mighty sick all the way down. He shouldn't ought to have been traveling."

"And he gave you a message."

"Yes, sir. He said I wasn't to tell it to anybody but you."

"Well, you have Dr. Johnson now, boy," Mr. Hamilton said.

I looked up at him, and then at General Washington, and finally at Dr. Johnson. "I ain't supposed to tell it to anybody but Dr. Johnson," I said, kind of low.

General Washington smiled. "All right, Arabus.

164

Come, gentlemen, let us leave these two to their business." Captain Ivers gave me a hard look, like he was warning me not to run off again, but he didn't dare go against General Washington. They all went out. Dr. Johnson sat down, and I stood in front of him and told him the whole message. Then he asked me a lot of questions about the message, just to make sure I'd got it right and wasn't lying about the whole thing.

"And how did you happen to meet Mr. Fatherscreft in the first place, Daniel?" he asked. "According to Captain Ivers, you jumped ship and ran away."

There wasn't any point in lying about that. "Yes, sir, I ran away. Captain Ivers, he was going to sell me off South."

"How do you know that?"

"I heard him tell Birdsey."

"Birdsey?"

"He's Captain Ivers's nephew," I said. "Or he was, sir. He got washed overboard in a storm on the way down."

"Yes, now I remember him. He was drowned?"

"Yes, sir."

"You've had a lot of hard luck recently, Daniel," he said.

"Yes, sir, I guess I have. Nor was that all of it." I reached into my shirt and took out the oilcloth package. "Captain Ivers is after my daddy's soldiers' notes."

"I don't understand."

So I told him all about it: how Mrs. Ivers had taken them from Mum, and how I'd stolen them back, and us planning on asking him to help us sell them so as to get our freedom money. He just sat there and listened and nodded, and asked a question here and there. When I got finished with the whole story, he said, "And you knew that Captain Ivers was in Philadelphia?"

"I reckoned he would be, knowing that me and Mr. Fatherscreft was headed that way," I said.

"And you came down anyway?"

"Yes, sir. I couldn't go back on a promise to a dying man."

He thought about it for a minute. Then he said, "You know, Daniel, I'm constantly surprised. It's generally said that Africans don't have a true moral sense, the same as whites do."

"Sir, I've been looking at the whole thing pretty hard the past little while, and it seems to me that there ain't much difference one way or another. You take my daddy, and Big Tom and Mr. Ivers and Birdsey and me, and take the skin off of us, and it would be pretty hard to tell which was the white ones and which ones wasn't."

"That's not what most white people believe."

"It ain't what most black folks believe, either. I didn't believe it myself, back home. But my daddy, he believed it, and I reckon I believe it now, myself."

166

He didn't say anything for another minute. Then he said, "Well now, Daniel, you understand that I have to turn you back to Captain Ivers. You're his property, and that's the law in Connecticut."

"I guess I know that as well as anybody," I said.

He gave me a sharp look to see if I was being uppity, but I wasn't sorry I'd said it. "I suppose you do," he said. "But did you know that it's also the law in Pennsylvania? However, I can see to it that he doesn't sell you for a while all right. Your father performed a service for the country, and now you've performed another one at considerable personal sacrifice. It's the least we can do. I'm sure that General Washington will agree with me, and I doubt strongly that Captain Ivers will want to oppose the general's wishes."

"Sir, I don't want to be uppity, but there's Mum."

"Oh, your mother, too." He smiled, then he got serious again. "Daniel, there's a lot of talk in Connecticut about passing a law forbidding the selling of slaves out of the state. I think such a law will pass, and if it does, you and your mother won't have to worry about being sold away."

"Sir, there's my daddy's soldiers' notes. Do you think they'll ever be worth anything?"

Dr. Johnson thought about that for a minute. "It's hard to predict," he said. "But I think they will. Now that we've got an agreement on the slavery question, I'm pretty confident we'll get a constitution to form a new nation with. And it's my belief that the new government will pay off the notes."

I could feel the tears come up behind my eyes, and I blinked to keep from crying. "So Mum and me could buy ourselves free?"

He thought about that some more. "Daniel, I think the smart thing would be for you to give me those notes for safekeeping. If the government votes to pay them off, I'll make an arrangement with Captain Ivers to obtain your freedom and your mother's."

And that was what happened. The next year, in 1788, Connecticut passed a law saying we couldn't be sold away from the state. The Constitution was voted on, too, and the thirteen colonies was organized into the United States. And soon the new government decided to pay off the soldiers' notes. Dr. Johnson took our notes to Captain Ivers and made a deal with him, and after that we were free. Oh, I can tell you, the day me and Mum packed out clothes and walked out of Captain Ivers's house was the greatest feeling I ever had. It was like the whole world for years and years had been in clouds, and then the sun came out.

We got a little cabin in Stratford where we could live. Mum went to work in Dr. Johnson's house, and I went to sea and began to save up money so I could buy my own fishing boat. It took five years but I did it, and after that things were a little easier, and Mum didn't have to work so hard. But we never forgot my daddy, for if it wasn't for him fighting all those years in the Revolution, we'd never have got free.

How Much of This Book Is True?

It is never easy, even for highly trained and experienced historians, to know exactly what happened in the past. We are always to some extent unsure about what we think we know. One of the things we are not sure about is how people spoke in the eighteenth century. We know how they wrote, of course, because we have many letters and diaries from that time. But we do not know if they talked the way they wrote.

Daniel Arabus almost certainly did not speak the way we have him talking in the book. The style of speech we have picked for him, and various other people, is much too modern for the Revolutionary Era. We have used this style in order to give the flavor of language as it might have been employed by a poor boy—black or white—without much schooling, growing up surrounded by people who did not speak English very well themselves.

In particular, we had to consider very carefully our use of the word *nigger*. This term is offensive to modern readers, and we certainly do not intend to be insulting. But it was commonly used in America right into the twentieth century, and it would have been a distortion of history to avoid its use entirely. In addition to historical accuracy, it was important to use the word to show how Daniel learned self-respect and developed self-confidence. You might also note which of the characters in the book used the term and which did not. Such use can tell you something about the social attitudes of the speakers.

Our story of what came to be known as the Constitutional Convention is taken from letters and diaries of the day. So are the details of American life, the villages, towns, and countryside as we have presented them. Daniel Arabus and his story, however, is fiction. A message of the kind he carried down to Philadelphia was indeed brought by somebody in order to bring about the compromise over slavery between those who favored it and those who opposed it. But we are not absolutely sure who carried the message or exactly what it said.

Peter Fatherscreft is also a fictional character. However, there were several people like him who were at the same time members of Congress and also of the Constitutional Convention and went back and forth between Philadelphia and New York. Philadelphia had a large population of Quakers who were leaders in the antislavery movement. Pennsylvania even today is known as the Quaker State. The little black girl whom Daniel called Nosy is also fictional, and so are such minor characters as the Trenton tavern keeper and Big Tom.

Captain Ivers is based on a real Captain Ivers who lived in Stratford, Connecticut, and sailed from the harbor there. We know very little about him, though, and most of the details of his life and character as they appear here are invented. However, we do know one thing about him; he owend a slave name Jack Arabus and sent him to serve in his place in the Revolution. Indeed, the whole story of Jack Arabus's service in the army for six or seven years, his return and Ivers's attempt to reenslave him, his jailing and his suit at law in New Haven, is entirely true and historically accurate as we have it here. The sketchy details we have are found in the official Connecticut law reports. The story of his friendship with Washing-

172

ton is borrowed from the life of another black Connecticut soldier named Samuel Bush. We do not know how or when Jack Arabus died, or whether he had a wife or children. That part is made up.

William Samuel Johnson, of course, is real. You can see his house today in Stratford. He was, in fact, a member of both the Congress in New York and the convention in Philadelphia at the same time. Later he was one of Connecticut's first senators under the new constitution. The little harbor of Newfield is now Bridgeport, Connecticut's, largest city. The Ivers's house we portray in this story still exists, preserved and moved to the grounds of the Bridgeport Museum of Art, Science and Industry. It was the house of Ivers's stepson, John Brooks, and you can visit it and walk around in it. The storm at sea is taken from Captain John Brooks's own journal of one of his voyages on the *Junius Brutus*. John Brooks and three of his sailors were actually washed off the deck, and Brooks and one sailor really were washed back on. You can read about it in his own handwriting in the journal preserved at the museum.

Black Sam Fraunces is also a historical character. Fraunces Tavern still exists in New York City, on Lower Manhattan. There is a restaurant there, and there is also a museum where you can see artifacts of Revolutionary times. The present building sits on the original foundation, but the

173

tavern burned down completely twice in the nine-teenth century. The current building was designed to be typical of the large inns of the eighteenth century, but we cannot be sure that the original tavern looked exactly as the present one does.

Sam Fraunces is quite an interesting character. He came from the West Indies in the 1750s and supplied food to the army during the Revolution, at which time he established a friendship with George Washington. Earlier he had purchased the tavern, which became one of the best-known inns in the United States. George Washington bade farewell to his officers at the end of the Revolution there. When Washington became our first president under the new Constitution, he asked Fraunces to serve as steward in his household. Actually, at the time of our story Fraunces had sold the tavern and was managing a farm in New Jersey, but he continued to have business interests in both Philadelphia and New York and visited the tavern quite frequently. Whether he knew Jack Arabus or not, we do not know; but the case of *Arabus* v. *Ivers* was well known among black Americans, and it is probable that he would have heard of it, at least.

Curiously, we are not sure whether Fraunces was in fact black. Trying to find out with certainty was one of the most interesting and intriguing re-search problems we encountered in writing this book. He was called Black Sam, and he did come from the West Indies, where there was a very large black population. Most modern writers have assumed that he was a black man—including several historians of colonial New York. However, the first United States census, which was taken in 1790, lists him as a "white male." It is our guess that he was of mixed blood. Perhaps he was part French, because his name was spelled Frances before he changed it—probably to conform to the way it was pronounced. Or maybe he was simply a dark-skinned white man.

Historians disagree about the major compromises of the Constitutional Convention. For years most historians believed that the disagreement most difficult to resolve was that of whether to give the most populous states more representatives and votes than the least populous states. That problem was solved by the Connecticut Compromise, which gives each state two senators no matter what their population is, but gives them a number of members of the House of Representatives proportionate to their population. During the past generation, however, through new research and study, many historians have come to see the slavery question as most important. Some say that the people of the United States missed their best opportunity to abolish slavery in 1787. Others say that was impossible given the conditions and attitudes of the time. In any event, we do know that the compromise described in our story did come about, and probably as a result of messages between the convention and Congress. Of course, we also know that slaves became more numerous and slave conditions became worse after the new government came into being. Finally, seventy-eight years after the days of our story, slavery was abolished as a result of a terrible Civil War.

This book, then, is a mixture of fact and fiction. We have tried, however, to capture a feeling of what it was like to live at the time this nation was being put together by the Founding Fathers.